"This character seems a lot like Iska…"

Aliceliese Lou Nebulis IX
Second princess of the Nebulis Sovereignty. Ordered by Mirabella to attend betrothal meetings.

"Mother! I haven't even had a boyfriend yet! It's much too soon to meet someone with marriage in mind!"

"Lady Alice, please give up."

Rin Vispose

Though she is part of the palace guards, she is also Alice's attendant and an unusual astral mage. She scolds Alice into going to betrothal meetings, but then…?

Mirabella Lou Nebulis VIII

The queen. Mother to Alice and her two sisters. Concerned about whether Alice has a boyfriend. ※The first and third sisters have already escaped from her.

"As a seventeen-year-old princess, you really should find a boyfriend. The palace is in agreement about this matter. In fact, it is a royal decree."

Our Last Crusade OR THE RISE OF A New World
Secret File

CONTENTS

File 01

Our Last Crusade or the
Double Booking Duel

001

File 02

Our Last Crusade or the
Unavoidable Clash at the
Bootcamp?

033

File 03

Our Last Crusade or Life in
a Flower Garden of Women

071

File 04

Our Last Crusade or Alice's
Betrothal War (Her Happily
Ever After)?

103

File XX

Our First Meeting

137

Secret

Or the Reunion the World
Knows Not Of

167

Afterword

175

Our Last CRUSADE OR THE RISE OF A New World

Secret File

1

KEI SAZANE

Illustration by
Ao Nekonabe

NEW YORK

Our Last CRUSADE OR THE RISE OF A New World

Secret File 1 KEI SAZANE

Translation by Jan Cash
Cover art by Ao Nekonabe

KIMI TO BOKU NO SAIGO NO SENJO, ARUIWA SEKAI GA HAJIMARU SEISEN Secret File Vol. 1
©Kei Sazane, Ao Nekonabe 2020
First published in Japan in 2020 by KADOKAWA CORPORATION, Tokyo.
English translation rights arranged with KADOKAWA CORPORATION, Tokyo, through TUTTLE-MORI AGENCY, INC., Tokyo.

English translation © 2023 by Yen Press, LLC

Yen On
150 West 30th Street, 19th Floor
New York, NY 10001

Visit us at yenpress.com
facebook.com/yenpress
twitter.com/yenpress
yenpress.tumblr.com
instagram.com/yenpress

First Yen On Edition: July 2023
Edited by Yen On Editorial: Shella Wu, Maya Deutsch
Designed by Yen Press Design: Liz Parlett

Yen On is an imprint of Yen Press, LLC.
The Yen On name and logo are trademarks of Yen Press, LLC.

The publisher is not responsible for websites (or their content) that are not owned by the publisher.

Cataloging in Publication data is on file with the Library of Congress.

ISBNs: 978-1-9753-4429-0 (paperback)
       978-1-9753-4430-6 (ebook)

10 9 8 7 6 5 4 3 2 1

LSC-C

Printed in the United States of America

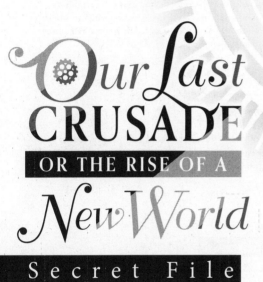

Our Last CRUSADE
OR THE RISE OF A
New World
Secret File

So Es lu, sis lavia.
You shall meet.

Ee yum soliin-Ye-ckt-kamyu bis xin peqqy.
You shall pass each other without remembering this time.

Lu Ee nex xedelis. Miqs, lu Ee tis-dia lan Zill qelno.
You need not think back to it. Right now, continue to walk straight toward the future.

THE HEAVENLY EMPIRE

Iska

Member of Unit 907—Special Defense for Humankind, Third Division. Used to be the youngest soldier who ever reached the highest rank in the military, the Saint Disciples. Stripped of his title for helping a witch break out of prison. Wields a black astral sword to intercept astral power and its white counterpart to reproduce the last attack obstructed by its pair. An honest swordsman fighting for peace.

Mismis Klass

The commander of Unit 907. Baby-faced and often mistaken for a child, but actually a legal adult. Klutzy but responsible. Trusts her subordinates. Became a witch after plunging into a vortex.

Jhin Syulargun

The sniper of Unit 907. Prides himself on his deadly aim. Can't seem to shake off Iska, since they trained under the same mentor. Cool and sarcastic, though he has a soft spot for his buddies.

Nene Alkastone

Chief mechanic of Unit 907. Weapon-making genius. Mastered operation of a satellite that releases armor-piercing shots from a high altitude. Thinks of Iska as her older brother. Wide-eyed and loveable.

Risya In Empire

Saint Disciple of the fifth seat. Genius-of-all-trades. A beautiful woman often seen in a suit and glasses with dark green frames. Likes Mismis, her former classmate.

THE NEBULIS SOVEREIGNTY

Aliceliese Lou Nebulis IX

Second-born princess of Nebulis. Leading candidate for the next queen. Strongest astral mage, who attacks with ice. Feared by the Empire as the Ice Calamity Witch. Hates all the backstabbing happening in the Sovereignty. Enraptured by fair fights against Iska, an enemy swordsman she met on the battlefield.

Rin Vispose

Alice's attendant. An astral mage controlling earth. Maid uniform conceals weapons for assassination. Skilled at deadly espionage. Hard to read her expressions, but has an inferiority complex about her chest.

Mirabella Lou Nebulis VIII

The queen. Mother to Alice and her two sisters. A veteran who has been in charge of multiple battles. Seems to have history with Salinger, the transcendental sorcerer...

Secret File

File 01

Our Last Crusade or the
Double Booking Duel

Our Last CRUSADE OR THE RISE OF A New World
Secret File

CONFIDENTIAL

Treaty of Friendship City, Köln.

The city had issued a request to the Imperial capital after the ancient Köln museum was set aflame and its treasure was stolen. Astral energy readings had also been detected on the scene.

The city believed a group of powerful witches and sorcerers were behind the operation, so they issued a plea for help.

"I know who did it! The thief who robbed the museum was none other than...Iska! It has to be *you*!" Mismis shouted.

Iska did not humor her outburst with a response.

"Ha-ha-ha. What do you think? Have my expert powers of deduction floored you?"

"I'm so shocked I don't even know what to say—that's the stupidest thing I've heard," Iska, the black-haired boy, replied with a sigh at his commander's accusation. "Commander Mismis, may I remind you that I'm part of the support unit that came here with you in order to catch the culprit..."

"How naive you are, my dear Iska! So naive!" Mismis strongly shook her head. "At times like these, the person you least suspect is always the culprit. That means you have to be the criminal since you came here to catch them!"

"By that logic, wouldn't you be the culprit, Commander Mismis?"

"What?"

"Well, you *are* my boss. And the Imperial Army dispatched you here to catch the perpetrator—plus, if we're going to follow the usual pattern of who's most suspicious, usually it's the woman rather than the man."

Commander Mismis Klass fell silent.

Though one could mistake her for a teenager, she was actually a full-grown adult who served as a commander in the Empire, the largest military state in the world. She led Unit 907 of the Special Division for Humankind, Third Division. Iska was also part of this unit.

"You're right…," Commander Mismis nodded as she replied, looking terribly serious. "You're analysis is spot-on. I must seem the most suspicious."

"Right?"

"But you're still the culprit, Iska."

"How does that make sense?!"

"Kidding! I just wanted to say that." Commander Mismis's voice was cheerful. She seemed to be enjoying this. "The case files of the great detective Mismis. What do you think? Maybe I'll start a new career once I leave the Imperial forces."

"…Sure," Iska said, but he really hoped she wouldn't.

He stopped himself just as he was about to point out that she would accuse people of crimes on a whim. Instead, he swallowed his words and glanced up at the clock tower.

4

"It looks like we've spent enough time hanging around now. We need to get going soon, Commander."

"It's almost time to meet, then. We need to make our way to the rendezvous, too."

"So, the stolen object was some sort of ancient treasure?"

"That's right. This city has a lot of excavation sites, but the robbers are a group of infamous witches and sorcerers who're supposed to be pretty dangerous. That's why they need our support— the Imperial forces' support, that is."

Commander Mismis started walking down the road. "Oh, look there. That's the museum."

They were in the city of Köln. The region had remained neutral over the course of the century-long war between the great nations of the Heavenly Empire and the Nebulis Sovereignty.

The beautiful streets were picture-perfect for sightseeing and served as popular tourist destinations, and they had been attacked by a group of robbers just the day before.

"Say, Iska, do you see how that building's all burned up on one side? Apparently, someone broke through the back door and stole the treasure while everyone was focused on the blaze."

"So it must have been some sort of flame astral power?"

"They detected astral energy from the cinders, which means the thieves are witches and sorcerers, too."

Commander Mismis carried a taser at her hip, a weapon the Imperial forces used to fight off and apprehend the vicious witches.

"According to what HQ told me, these sorts of incidents with witches are advantageous for the Empire. If we fight off villains like them, other nations will trust us more, strengthening our diplomatic ties."

"That would make things easier in the war against the Nebulis Sovereignty." Iska nodded as he looked up at the museum.

It had happened a century ago. On one fateful day, the Empire, which once maintained hegemony over the world, had discovered astral power, the forbidden energy source that lay dormant within the planet.

When astral powers possessed a human being, it gave them powers straight out of a fairy tale. Owing to their fearful and dangerous abilities, women with astral power were called witches, while men were called sorcerers.

The Empire had identified them as threats and ousted them from the nation.

On the other hand...

The witches had sought refuge from the Empire's persecution and created a country of their own—the witch's paradise, the Nebulis Sovereignty.

"Well...It's one thing for them to send out the Imperial forces, but...," Commander Mismis let out a sigh. "HQ is being so mean to us. They said to only send out the bare minimum of personnel. I know we don't have enough soldiers out to fight on the battlefront, but we're dealing with a band of witches. We're definitely going to be in danger, too."

"I'll make up for that," Iska said.

"I'm sorry, Iska. I know I'm going to be relying on you a lot."

"You should. I'll take the lead when we need to fight, so just focus on giving instructions, Commander."

He was a witch-hunting swordsman, unusual in that he only used blades to fight in close combat despite being from a mechanically advanced nation renowned for its firearms.

That was Iska.

He had once been selected to serve as a Saint Disciple, the direct guard of the Empire's Lord, and was considered one of the foremost experts in anti-witch combat techniques in their nation.

"But I can't guarantee that I'll be able to defeat them. You should stay on guard when things get heated, too, Commander. That's how dangerous these people are."

Even Iska had a difficult time fighting against powerful witches. One particular example came to mind—and that fight had ended without a conclusive winner.

...I guess Alice is the one I'd think of.

...Since her powers are on a whole other level.

The Imperial forces called her the Ice Calamity Witch, and they had declared her an enemy of the state. As Iska thought of the witch in the back of his mind, he shook his head.

"Anyway, Commander Mismis, I'm not seeing the person we're supposed to meet up with."

"Same here. I'm also keeping an eye out for them. We need to get in contact with them since the city assembly asked the Imperial forces for help."

The two of them continued to scan the area.

Right at that moment...

"Rin, you're sure we're to meet the assembly member here, right?"

"Yes, Lady Alice. I believe that museum is the building that was damaged. We are to meet in front of it."

Iska and Mismis heard approaching footsteps, accompanied by the shared whispers of two young women.

"A robbery committed by astral mages...how terrible. Their abuse of their powers is a disgrace to us all. People might even start calling entirely unrelated mages, like us, witches and sorcerers because of this."

"I'm sure the thieves were mages who were banished from the Sovereignty."

"How unforgivable. It is a grave crime for any Sovereignty

mages to attack other nations. On my honor as a Nebulis princess, I must catch them!"

Her voice grew staunch from sheer anger.

...Huh? That voice.

...I think I recognize it.

Iska thought it sounded oddly familiar.

"Hey, Iska? I feel like I recognize that voice."

Commander Mismis tilted her head in befuddlement.

Just then, Mismis and a young blond woman bumped shoulders as they passed each other.

"Ah!"

"Oh, I'm so sorry! I wasn't looking where I was walking...!"

Commander Mismis bowed frantically even though they only brushed each other at most.

"Are you all right?"

"Thank you for the concern. I'm sorry I wasn't paying enough attention either."

The blond girl gave a charming bow. She was about the same age as Iska, with a sweet, adorable face and a healthy and well-developed figure.

"Well, if you'll excuse—"

The young woman stopped in her tracks—but she wasn't looking at Commander Mismis now. Instead, she practically froze the moment she saw Iska behind the commander.

"......Huh?"

"Huh? There's no way..."

Iska gulped when he saw the young lady.

They knew each other. Well, that wasn't exactly the right way of putting it. After all, the two of them had fought each other on a distant battlefield and were mortal enemies.

"Alice?!"

"Iska?!"

They both pointed at each other and yelled each other's names.

Aliceliese Lou Nebulis IX. As a princess of the witch's paradise, the Nebulis Sovereignty, she possessed formidable astral power. She was also known as the Ice Calamity Witch. She was strong enough to destroy an entire Imperial military base single-handedly, and she'd fought Iska to a draw at his full strength. Now they were rivals.

"What are you doing here, Alice?"

"I should be asking you that! What are you doing here...and why are you with your superior from the Imperial forces?!"

Alice's eyes widened when she realized who she had run into. Even Commander Mismis was dumbfounded to have run into such an infamous witch.

Not to mention it was an awkward situation. Though they were in a neutral city, they had run right into an enemy.

"Please move back, Lady Alice!"

Rin, Alice's attendant, stepped in front of the princess to protect her. In addition to her formidable astral power, Rin had also been trained in the arts of assassination and hand-to-hand combat.

"Imperial swordsman...so you appear before us again!" She didn't even bother to hide her animosity. "You've been tailing Lady Alice, then. Fine. I shall take Lady Alice's place, and this time I will make sure this breath will be your—"

"Wait, Rin."

Alice bid her attendant to stop just as Rin was pulling a knife from her skirt.

"This is a neutral city. We can't fight here, even against Imperials."

"B-but..."

"Besides, astral mages have already stirred up trouble here. What good will it do causing another incident?"

"……Of course."

"There you have it, Iska. Alas, I think we won't have the time to settle our fight." Alice sighed in disappointment. "I can't tell you many details since you're an Imperial soldier, but some trouble occurred in this city. I'm afraid I'm terribly busy trying to resolve the issue."

"You don't mean the robbery at the museum over there, do you?"

"Huh?" Alice widened her eyes and blinked. "How do you know about that?"

"Commander Mismis and I were asked to catch the thieves."

"They asked *you* to come *here*?" The Nebulis princess fixed him with a stare. "Wait. That's impossible. How could a neutral city request aid from both the Sovereignty and the Empire! It's unheard of!"

Alice was right. The two countries were at war. It was too much to ask for the two nations to combine forces in order to apprehend the robbers.

"Iska, listen carefully." Alice took a step forward. "A group of astral mages are responsible for this scandal. So it stands to reason that I, a princess of the astral mages, should clear our names. There's no need for you to be here."

"Of course there is." Iska was direct with his response. "Astral mages committed this crime. It makes sense we'd lend the city our aid, considering we have tons of experience battling them."

"No! We cannot allow the Imperial forces to bolster their reputation!" Alice placed a hand on her ample bosom. "*I* accepted the city's request!"

11

"B-but! We received a formal summons from the city and were sent here by the Imperial headquarters, too!" Commander Mismis retorted. "Did *you* actually receive a request?"

"Of course!" Rin spoke up. "Did *you* actually—"

"Oh…say, Rin, isn't he the one who asked us to come here?" Alice cut her attendant off.

A man wearing a suit had stepped out of the damaged museum. He was rather young to be an assembly member, seeming timid and methodical. Honestly, he looked more like someone's secretary than an official.

"Gracious! I apologize for the wait. I'm Domperi, one of the assemblymen…!" He bowed low, first turning his eyes to look at Commander Mismis. "Thank you, um…"

"I'm Commander Mismis, dispatched from the Imperial forces. And this is one of my subordinates, Iska. You can count on us now that we're here!" Mismis thumped her chest as she said that. "I won't do much work, but Iska sure will."

"Uh, Commander, I think you'll need to help out, too?"

"Ha-ha-ha. Thank you very much. Your composure is reassuring, in a way!" Domperi said, his voice ringing out. Then he turned to Alice and Rin. "Why, hello. And you must be, um…"

"We have arrived from the Nebulis Sovereignty. I am the Second Princess Aliceliese." Alice politely bowed. "I am very sorry for the problems you've faced. Our nation shall compensate you for damages to the museum and medical fees for the injured."

"You're royalty?! I can't believe a *princess* from the Nebulis Sovereignty is here!"

His eyes went wide. His reaction was only natural, of course. The princess of one of the two largest nations in the world had personally made her way to a remote city. On top of that, she was a very beautiful woman, which made his effervescence all the more understandable.

"Please rest assured. We will take responsibility and capture the culprit. You can count on us."

"It would be an honor, Princess Alice!" The man exchanged a firm handshake with Alice.

Mismis was quick to react. "Excuse me!"

She placed herself between the two. "There's something wrong here! Mr. Domperi, you asked the Empire for help, didn't you?!"

"Why, of course!" He nodded firmly.

Then Rin cut in. "Mr. Domperi, I believe you called upon the Sovereignty for assistance as well?"

"Yes, indeed. We asked you for help capturing the astral mage thieves... Oh my?"

It seemed he'd finally realized the situation.

Iska and Commander Mismis were to his right. Alice and Rin were to the left. He looked at each group of individuals, whose two nations had very different ideals.

"The Empire...and the Sovereignty...yes, there is something wrong here. I asked two secretaries to make calls to the country we can count on for help. Oh no. They couldn't have..."

"Rin, I think I understand what's happened." A rarely seen, strained smile spread across Alice's face. "He says he has two secretaries. They both must have called in anyone they knew who could fight in order to catch the robbers. I can understand why they panicked."

"Yes, Lady Alice. So one must have called the Sovereignty, and the other requested help from the Empire."

"What? But that's a terrible idea...," Commander Mismis quietly murmured, dumbfounded. "Isn't it, Iska?"

"Basically, this is a double booking. That's really the worst thing they could have done. I can't believe they asked for help from both the Empire and the Sovereignty."

"What?!" The man instantly went pale in the face. "I can't believe my secretaries would call two countries at war to meet at the same place… Yikes! You're not going to fight here, are you?!"

"Oh, no, it's fine. Please calm down," Iska quickly mollified the assemblyman.

"This is a neutral city. The Empire and Sovereignty are forbidden from fighting here, even if we run into each other," Alice added.

"I…I see…"

"That's right. We're well aware of that, too." Iska nodded and signaled to Alice with his eyes.

That's how it is.

Yes. I have no qualms about that.

Iska could tell from Alice's expression that she agreed.

Though then again, Iska and Alice had already met in a neutral city before. They'd even dined at the same table, in fact.

…It's similar to what happened back then, anyway.

…I'm used to bumping into her in random places like this.

Whenever they were in a neutral city, they would lay down their arms. They were quite accustomed to it at this point.

"But there is one important matter we have yet to discuss." Alice crossed her arms, her eyes showing she was restraining herself. "Which one of us will take on this request? We need to make that clear."

"Yeah, we really should."

They'd both been called in. One of them would have to withdraw.

The Sovereignty should back out.

The Empire ought to step down.

Iska and Alice locked eyes.

"Listen, Iska." Alice walked forward. "The robbers are mages who gathered after being ousted by the Sovereignty. It's my duty as princess to capture them if they've run amok."

"No, it's an Imperial soldier's job to protect the populace from nefarious astral mages."

Iska did not back down even slightly. They'd been formally ordered to carry out this mission by their headquarters, so he and Mismis couldn't simply withdraw.

More important, they both felt that if they ran away here, they'd be losing to the other's stubbornness.

They silently stared each other down.

"Well, in any case, we shouldn't waste our time here." Alice sighed in resignation. "I'll acknowledge that we're at fault for giving the Empire a pretext to intervene, so here's the best concession I can make—let's have a fair and square competition."

"You mean to see who captures the culprits?"

"Yes. But capturing them won't solve this, so we must go after the leader. So, let's say whoever catches that person will receive all the credit?"

"I'm fine with that. What do you think, Commander Mismis?"

"Sure, I'm okay with it, too," Commander Mismis also seemed amenable to the agreement.

It was a realistic compromise, and they wouldn't be defying headquarters' orders this way.

"Then it's settled." Alice lightly brushed aside her bangs and looked at the man. "Well, sir, if you could please tell us where the robbers went…and if you could also prepare a car. Rin is able to drive, so you do not need to worry."

"Yes, I'll gladly leave things to you!...The only problem is that we have just one car."

"What?" Alice's eyes went wide, and she blinked. "Meaning...?"

"We prepared a special armored vehicle...but I'm afraid we were only able to procure one." His voice petered out. "...I wasn't aware we had called two nations to help us."

"Uh, well, that seems like a problem, don't you think, Iska?" Mismis crossed her arms, looking troubled. "There's only one car, and we came here by an Imperial bus, so we don't have another vehicle either..."

"Sometimes concessions have to be made," Iska said. "If neither of us are going to give up the car, we have only one option."

He looked at Alice, who was right in front of him. Iska honestly felt awkward about the situation, but if they didn't hurry, the robbers would get away. In other words, they would need to share the car.

"Alice."

"What a coincidence...Yes, I'd come to the same conclusion as well," Alice matter-of-factly replied. Or rather—she turned away somewhat awkwardly.

"Y-you do realize though, Iska, that this will be the first and last time that I will share a ride with an Imperial like you!"

———

Outskirts of Köln.

An armored vehicle rushed through the tall woodland trees.

"Iska, it's this way, right?"

"Yes. I see a large forest to the right of us. The witnesses reported seeing the robbers flee to north of the woods."

Mismis sat in the driver's seat. Iska, meanwhile, was in the back seat, scanning a map as he gave her directions.

"Their hideout might be in the woods."

"Then we'll keep heading north!" Commander Mismis quickly jerked the steering wheel. She was so caught up that she slammed on the acceleration.

"Um, so…," Mismis nervously managed to say as she eyed the knife that was pointed at her from the corner of her eyes. "I *can* go faster, right?"

"I'll permit it," Rin, who happened to be pointing said knife at Mismis, answered coldly. "But don't forget. Lady Alice is riding with us. If you so much as look like you're doing something suspicious, I will run this dagger straight through you."

"I'm not going to do anything! I'm not doing anything suspicious at all!"

Out of all the things that could have happened, they'd both been called to this city and ended up in the same car. Commander Mismis was driving, and Rin was keeping an eye on her from the passenger seat.

"Ow, ow! You realize you've been poking me in the shoulder with the knife, right?!"

"It's because you're not driving smoothly enough. How suspicious…so you *are* up to something, aren't you?!"

"That's only happening because you keep poking me! Aghhh! Help me, Iska! Your superior officer is in trouble!"

"I really would like to help, but…"

Though he could see why his commander was begging for help, Iska had his own reasons for not being able to move. He was right next to a blond young lady who was sitting regally in her seat.

"I can't move either," Iska finished.

"What exactly is that supposed to mean?"

Alice turned to the side. Though the vehicle was rather large, because of the reinforced armor, the back seats were a snug fit for two people.

"Say, Alice, could you scoot over a little more?"

"I'd like to ask you to do the same. I think you could stand to use a little less space."

"I have my swords with me, though."

Iska was a swordsman at his core. He'd placed the two blades he always carried with him against a corner of his seat.

"I think you've got more room on your side, Alice."

"Of course I don't. I have just the same amount as you... See!"

Alice half rose up from her seat.

She had only done that to compare the amount of space she had compared to Iska's...

"Ah! I see the car!" Mismis abruptly hit the brakes. The entire vehicle lurched, and Alice fell over from her standing position.

"Ah!"

"Eep?!"

The Nebulis princess fell right into his arms, her ample chest pressing into Iska's face. Something plump hit his cheek.

"Ahhh?! Iska, what do you think you've buried your face into?!"

"You're the one who fell onto *me*, Alice! Would you move out of the way...!"

Iska gently shoved Alice aside to move her off him. Or at least he thought he did. Just then, he realized that he'd found purchase on her bare thigh, which was sticking out from under her skirt.

"*Now* where do you think you're touching?!"

"Th-this is all a misunderstanding!"

"What's there to misunderstand about your hand being right *there*?!"

Alice had turned red right up to her ears.

It wasn't an exaggeration to say her beauty was practically un-rivaled and no one—not even anyone from the Empire—would have believed she was a witch when witnessing her charm from so close. Alas, Iska didn't have time to bask in the experience.

"Iska, you oaf! You're shameless!"

"I'm telling you that I just caught you when you fell, Alice!"

"That's entirely irrelevant!"

She shrieked and screamed from the back seat.

"Iska, pipe down a little."

"Lady Alice, we're in the robber's territory. Though we are in the car, I believe we will have a problem if they hear your shouts."

"Yes, ma'am…"

"Right…"

Both Mismis and Rin glared sharply at the two. Iska and Alice exchanged looks.

"It's your fault Rin scolded me."

"Well, it's *your* fault I got in trouble with the Commander, Alice."

They were at the edge of a gloomy forest.

"Rin, you're sure it's this car?"

"Yes, Lady Alice. In all likelihood, I believe it is the one that the culprits used for their escape."

Alice and Rin were pointing at a vehicle parked in the shade of the trees. Commander Mismis had braked so suddenly because she spotted the robber's car.

"Wow, Commander, you did great." Iska admired the feat. She'd found it despite how deftly it had been hidden. "I'm impressed you spotted it. It's in the shade and hidden in the bushes, so it's hard to make out."

"Hee-hee. Well, I suppose that's just years of experience for you." Mismis grinned bashfully. "You know how the capital doesn't have any parking spaces, right? I've gotten really good at finding illegal parking spots that people can't see, so I know pretty much every place someone would hide a vehicle."

"That seems like some pretty scummy real-world experience!"

"Oh, don't get me wrong. I don't do it anymore. I used to get up to no good with that when I was younger."

"...Really?"

In any case, she'd still managed to find the car. The robbers likely hadn't imagined that it'd be spotted either.

"Rin, do you think they're deeper in the woods?"

"Yes. It would be a reasonable location for their hideout. But I think it will be very difficult to find."

They couldn't see farther than a few meters ahead due to the vegetation blocking their view. They would need to walk through the woods to continue their search.

"Iska, you know what we need to do, don't you?"

She stomped on a protruding rock. Alice, the Ice Calamity Witch, turned to look into the depths of the silent woods.

"I don't think we need to work together anymore. We're no longer in the neutral city and the two of us are enemies, so we really *can't* work together." Her tone was firm, as she was a princess from an enemy nation. "Isn't that right?"

"Right."

He met her gaze directly. If anything, Iska had been waiting for an appropriate time to mention it himself. Though they were after the same target, they had no intention of working together.

From here on, the competition would begin.

"We'll go about this just as we discussed earlier." Alice pointed at the tree-lined animal trails.

"The robbers who stole the treasure are somewhere in these woods," she said.

"I know. And whoever captures their leader gets the credit, right?"

It was winner-take-all. Whoever apprehended the robbers would receive all the reward money and honor.

"We'll part ways here."

"Okay. Then we'll take the path on the right," Iska said, signaling at Commander Mismis before walking that direction.

"Rin, let's go. We'll search the one on the left."

Alice and Rin headed off into the thickets.

"......Right. This finally feels like a real mission!"

Commander Mismis seemed nervous as she produced her gun—an Imperial-issued taser rather than a real gun since they aimed to capture the criminals this time. That said, the taser was set for the highest possible output so it would be combat-ready. It could take out a bear with a single shot if used at point-blank range.

"Iska, I'll tell you this now..."

"Yes?"

"I'm apologize in advance if I hit you from behind with this taser."

"What are you talking about?!"

"Uh, well, when I get nervous, my aim tends to be off."

"...Please don't make excuses *before* you've even shot me."

It really wasn't anything to laugh about. In reality, about thirty percent of battlefield injuries were the result of friendly fire from behind.

"I'll hold on to your gun, then."

"Hey! Wait!!"

"You've already done enough, Commander. You spotted the robber's car." He brushed aside a tree branch and continued into the dark woods. "It's my turn to shine from here. In order to capture the leader of the robbers, we need to find their hideout first."

"And before the two of them."

"If they find it, they'll definitely apprehend the leader first."

"...Yeah, they would. She's the Ice Calamity Witch, after all."

She'd supposedly destroyed an entire Imperial base single-handedly. Though witches themselves, the robbers wouldn't stand a chance against her.

"Okay, then we really need to psych ourselves up!" Commander Mismis continued to push her way through the thickets. "You should be careful too, Iska. If this is near the thieves' hideout, they might've set up traps!"

"Commander, there's a sharp twig right in front of your eyes."

"What? Oh! Ouch!!"

A branch with prickles as sharp as the prongs of a fork hit the commander square in the forehead.

"See, don't just keep your eyes on your feet."

"Aggghh..." Tears welled up in her eyes. Mismis stopped in her tracks and blinked. "Oh, say, Iska..."

"Commander, watch out for the branches."

"No, not that. Look over there. Doesn't that look like the dark brown fabric of a tent?"

"What?"

He looked toward where she pointed.

From between the gaps of the thickly grown trunks, he could see a camouflaged dome-like tent peeking through. It was a familiar sight—the camping tents used by the Nebulis Sovereignty during guerrilla warfare. This was undoubtedly the robbers' hideout.

"What? That's amazing, Commander..."

"Oh, it wasn't much! Looks like all that illegal parking really did sharpen my observation skills."

"I'm not so sure about that...but this doesn't seem good. Looks like there are more of them than we anticipated."

There were five tents in total, so there were fourteen—maybe even fifteen—robbers.

The group was large enough to even be a full unit within the Nebulis Sovereignty's astral corps. There weren't so many that Iska couldn't handle them, but if he spent too long taking care of the underlings, the leader might have time to escape.

...What do I do?

...Is it safer to observe them for a while first?

He waited for an opening from the shadows of a tree. Then the thickets quivered right before their eyes.

"Lady Alice, we've found it. This must be the robbers' hideout."

"Good work, Rin. I knew you would find it!"

Immediately after her, a blond girl in brilliant garments appeared out of the thickets.

"I'm sure Iska isn't here yet. Well, the early bird gets the worm!"

"There do seem to be more robbers than we anticipated, however, Lady Alice," said Rin, surveying the camouflaged tents while standing in front of her. "Shall we observe them?"

"No, we'll attack." Alice majestically, with utmost elegance, leaped out from the bushes. "I can't let Iska beat me. Before he arrives—"

"I'm already here."

"Yes, you're already here...... Wait, Iska?!" Alice flinched and moved back. "Grr...you put up a good fight. Well, the one who apprehends the leader wins, just as we agreed. And I'll capture all the underlings too, of course!"

"I know," Iska assured her.

"Then let the games begin!" Alice's declaration rang throughout the woods. Naturally, the robbers heard her loud cry in their hideout as well.

"What was that noise?!"

"Is it someone after us from the city?!"

The witches and sorcerers ran out of their tents.

The clear marks on their arms and faces were astral crests—which were considered ominous marks within the Empire, and one reason why the witches and sorcerers were feared as monsters. Iska attacked one of the sorcerers without hesitation.

"An Imperial soldier?!"

There was a crimson crest on the man's shoulder.

He had flame astral power. After a quick glance, Iska leaped off the ground and sped up, silently charging forward. He leaped over a boulder and flung himself through the air overhead.

"Raging fire, awaken!"

Countless embers appeared from thin air, condensing together to form a gigantic orb that came crashing down over Iska's head. This was an astral power in action. The giant fireball had manifested almost like magic.

"It won't work."

A black blade flashed. With one wave of the sword in his hand, Iska cut through the fire, and it vanished.

"My power...you *cut* through it?!"

"There's no astral power I can't cut through." Iska instantly passed through the remaining flames and headed straight for the sorcerer.

"Why you little—"

"Too slow." Iska didn't even give the man time to finish as he elbowed him right in the chest.

The sorcerer collapsed to the ground.

At the same time, the screams of several witches echoed throughout the woods behind Iska.

"Lady Aliceliese?!"

"Wh-what are you doing here?!"

They weren't crying out in *surprise*. They were screaming with *fear*, their faces pale.

The witches were frozen—literally. Three of them were encased in blocks of ice from the neck down and were effectively captured, unable to move a muscle.

"I'll tell you this now rather than later. I'm incredibly upset."

Alice's voice really did reflect her fury.

The witch princess—feared by the Imperial forces—cast a glance at the immobile witches before moving on.

"I cannot forgive any of you for the misdeeds you committed with your astral powers. You should know you won't be able to escape now that I've arrived. I simply have no time to deal with underlings like you."

She wasn't looking at them, but rather at the Imperial swordsman.

While Alice had frozen over the three witches, Iska had taken down two additional robbers. In other words, Iska had taken down three, and Alice had also taken down three. It had all happened in the blink of an eye.

"Impressive, Iska, but I won't let you take even one more of them from me."

"This *is* a competition, after all."

Alice's powers gave her the range advantage. But to compensate for that, Iska had the agility to run through the woods like the wind.

"Roar, crash of thunder!"

"Also too slow."

Iska cleared away the lightning arrows that assaulted both him and Alice. Using his sword, he sliced through the deluge of astral attacks coming for him so fast they were almost impossible to react to. At the same time, he ran toward the sorcerer. But just when he reached the mage...

"You're the one who's too slow."

Alice had already frozen the man solid before Iska made it.

"Looks like I've apprehended four now."

"That's cheating! I cleared away his lightning!"

"And *I* captured him. This is why they say the early bird gets the worm."

Hee-hee, Alice giggled mischievously. She looked to be genuinely enjoying herself. Her smile was hardly appropriate for someone meeting her mortal enemy on the battlefield.

"See, Iska. The next one is coming. Please ready your sword."

"Guh...that's unfair, Alice!"

Iska cleared away every single attack that came toward him with swipes of his sword, and Alice used those opportunities to freeze the witches each time. They were working together so harmoniously, but Alice continued to pick off his targets from the sidelines.

"They were supposed to be mine...!"

"Oh, but this is a competition, you realize? We're not working together, you know," Alice's voice rang out from behind Iska. "That makes six for me. And it seems you're stuck at three, Iska."

"No, the person who captures the leader wins."

Iska continued to run ahead of Alice. Since he had superior physical capabilities, he was at an advantage when it came to catching the leader. He just needed to keep this up until he overtook Alice to find them. However...

"That is odd. I don't see her...?" Alice said after stopping at the center of the five tents and searching her surroundings. "They say the ringleader was a female astral mage with black hair who looked like she was still in her teens. But I haven't seen her among the mages we've taken down so far."

"Me neither. She's not in the tents."

Iska had been slicing through the fabric of the tents and peering into them. He saw no sign of the ringleader, however. The woman didn't seem to be on the premises.

"Iska, dear, to your right!"

"Lady Alice, she ran from behind the tent into the woods!"

They both heard Commander Mismis and Rin yell simultaneously from a distance.

"So she's over there!"

The black-haired witch parted the dark thickets as she made a break for it. She was already difficult to spot, since she blended in with the foliage and underbrush.

...*This is bad.*

...*The visibility in the woods is already terrible. If she gets away here, we have no chance of catching her.*

And she was too far away to chase after.

"Iska, jump up!" He heard a call from behind.

Princess Alice addressed him in her dignified and tranquil voice.

"Ice Calamity. Hall of the Sacred Dance of the Midnight Moon."

His vision was flooded with snow that whipped around him in

27

the conjured wind. The ground froze before his eyes, which sped across the vegetation to pursue the witch.

"...Ice?!"

The witch widened her eyes when she saw the frost on the trees. Then vines of ice wrapped around her feet, and she tumbled forward. But on top of being the ringleader of the thieves, this girl was a respectable astral mage herself.

"Wind, smash it!"

A vortex tore away at the ice around her legs, and she quickly stood up.

"This is it."

"What?"

The Imperial swordsman cornered her at a tremendous speed.

Thump... With near mechanical precision, Iska gave a karate chop to the back of the girl's head.

Alice had attacked in order to keep the girl at bay. Even a few seconds would have been enough. She knew Iska would pursue the girl once she stopped the mage—and that faith in him had been the reason she'd been able to instantly come up with such a plan.

"Did you get her?"

"Yeah, she's unconscious."

Now that they'd apprehended the leader, the thieves' group had been dismantled.

Yes, under normal circumstances, this would have concluded with an "all's well that ends well," but reality wasn't that simple...

"Aren't I just wonderful! I caught the leader, so the whole issue's been resolved!"

"Wait a second."

As Alice proclaimed her victory, Iska stopped her.

"I was the one who caught the leader. I stopped her while she was trying to run away."

"What are you talking about? Just look around for yourself." Alice pointed at the ice on the ground. "I stopped her flight using my astral power. You never would have managed to apprehend her without me. In other words, this was my achievement and I've won!"

"But I was the one who actually caught her. You technically didn't do that."

"What!"

"Am I wrong?"

"No…I suppose you're right." Alice swept away her bangs with a graceful hand. "You never hesitate to argue with me, despite the fact that I'm a Nebulis Sovereignty princess. It's a great trait, but I also can't simply acquiesce."

"And by that you mean…"

"It's a duel!" Alice cried out as she pointed at him. "A rematch between you and me. We'll continue where we left off from last time when we had a draw!"

"I have no qualms with that."

"This is an excellent opportunity. I'll show you which one of us will win this time."

Iska readied his twin swords. Opposite him, Alice also prepared herself for battle.

"It's a rematch!" they both cried out simultaneously.

"Iska?!"

"Lady Alice!"

Commander Mismis and Rin were both shouting at them. Just as the two were ready to clash, their verve was easily swept aside.

"Iska, the city has sent in a reinforcement unit. They're a little late, though."

"Lady Alice? Is something the matter?"

"N-not at all!" Alice waved a panicked hand at Rin, who had

run up to her and then reluctantly backed away. The princess stared intently at Iska.

"...It seems we will be postponing this, as we've been interrupted."

She looked displeased, like a child who'd had an activity canceled because of the rain. She murmured in chagrin, her emotions stark on her face, "We'll consider this a draw. We'll hand over the robbers to the city's vigilance committee and allow them to pass judgement. Rin, let's go home."

"Oh, please wait, Lady Alice," Rin called to stop her. "We still have to go through the procedures of collecting the reward for capturing them."

"I don't need that." Alice turned around. The golden-haired witch faced Iska head-on and gave him a bitter smile. "The thieves were the Sovereignty's responsibility. Would you give them the reward to make up for the damage they caused from their crimes?"

"It sure sounds like you're asking me to do all the paperwork."

"A princess doesn't often involve herself with such formalities, besides..."

They heard footsteps approaching. The reinforcements were almost there.

"While it's one thing to be in a neutral city, the two of us can't be seen fraternizing outside of one for very long. We are enemies, after all."

The Ice Calamity Witch turned her back to him, her silky golden hair fluttering.

"So, while I'm somewhat reluctant to part ways, this will be all for today."

As she turned away, he caught her momentarily winking at him.

"See you later, Iska. Let's meet on the battlefield next time."

"......Right."

She headed out with her attendant in tow.

Iska stared at her from behind.

And then...as the fate of the planet would have it, the two would reunite with each other, but that will be a story for another time.

File 02

Our Last Crusade or the
Unavoidable Clash at the Bootcamp?

Secret File

Spring.

The freezing chill of winter ended, heralding the season for budding flowers. Cherry blossoms flitted about; birds sang. And during this joyous time of year...

"NOOoooo!"

The Imperial capital Yunmelngen.

In the third base of the Empire, the largest militarized nation in the world, Commander Mismis wailed.

"I don't wanna go! I don't wanna do bootcamp!"

She was lying on the floor of the conference room, flailing her arms and putting up the greatest resistance she could muster as she kept shouting, "No, no!"

The commander showed not a shred of embarrassment or concern for her integrity as she threw a tantrum like a child refusing to go to school.

"Commander Mismis, please calm down."

"...Iska?"

"Don't be scared. Come on, please get up." The Imperial

swordsman, Iska, addressed her in a soothing tone and offered his hand to his superior officer. "Please look out the window. There's a bright blue sky out today. Look, there are even birds over there by the base. It's such a nice time of year."

"Y-yeah, it is."

"Spring's right around the corner. Commander, what comes to mind during this season?"

"...Flower viewing?"

"For the Imperial forces, spring is synonymous with bootcamp."

"Nooooo!!"

It was no use.

He'd tried to make bootcamp out to be another tiding of the season, but it seemed Mismis harbored a repulsion for the very word.

"You don't need to be so dramatic. We're not even doing submarine or aircraft training. It's just the basics, like running laps and strength work."

"Those are the things I'm worst at. You should know that, Iska..."

Commander Mismis looked deflated.

Despite her behavior, she was actually a full-grown adult at the age of twenty-two, but with her cherubic face, combined with her short stature, she could pass as a kid who recently graduated elementary school.

"Commander, as I remember it, you just barely managed to meet the required height for the Imperial forces, correct?"

"That's right. I passed by wearing really thick socks that added two centimeters."

"That's definitely against regulations!"

"Back then I was convinced I had some more height in me. But that's not the issue at hand, Iska!" Still sprawled on the ground,

Mismis pointed at herself. "All the members of the forces are huge and muscular. But the Imperial bootcamp even leaves those tough guys in the dust. And you want an itty-bitty lady like me to go to *that*?!"

"I sympathize with your pain…"

Bootcamp—which was generally known as "basic training and combat" or BTC—struck fear into the hearts of many Imperial force members on an annual basis.

"It must be a cakewalk for you though, Iska," Mismis said.

"No, no. It was like hell back when I first enlisted."

Even Iska, who'd had the greatest swordsman in the Empire as his teacher, had almost given up during BTC when he first joined the forces. He'd been thrown into a pool with his hands tied, and he'd been forced to seal himself for two minutes in a room filled with tear gas without a gas mask and collapsed because he hadn't been able to breathe. That was how unreasonable their training was.

"But luckily, Special Division III's bootcamp only lasts a week."

"I still don't wanna goooo!" Commander Mismis screeched again.

"Let her be, Iska. She's just up to her typical antics." Jhin, the silver-haired sniper reclining in a folding chair in a corner of the room, turned to them. "It's the same as how a cicada starts buzzing once summer rolls around. Whenever spring bootcamp comes, the boss always starts wailing. It's just more of her usual stuff."

"Oh, Jhin, isn't that a terrible thing to compare her to. How could you basically call her a cicada?" Nene asked.

She was sitting next to Jhin, her red hair done up in a ponytail.

That was everyone. Mismis was in charge of Iska, Jhin, and Nene, who all made up Unit 907.

"Look at this, Jhin." Nene pointed at Commander Mismis,

who was still lying on the ground. "A cicada buzzes for its future. That's completely different from Commander Mismis, since she's crying in order to avoid training. Lumping her together with the cicadas does them a disservice!"

"You're so mean, Nene!" Mismis couldn't let that go, of course, and leaped up. "Well, if you're going as far to say that about your superior officer, that puts me in an awkward position. Well, Iska, when's the bootcamp, then?"

"Right, we actually just got word about that." Iska produced a notice from his pocket and handed it to the commander. "It starts tomorrow."

"You've got to be kidding!"

"They announce it without warning every year, after all."

"But it's still ridiculous... Aww, I had plans during my time off this week, too."

Mismis turned to look up at the ceiling.

Just then, the conference room door flung open with a *Bam*.

"Keep it down! We can hear your wailing in the next room over!...Wait, is that you, Commander Mismis?"

A bespectacled, black-haired commanding officer walked right into the room. Though she had a serious air about her, she curled her lips into a mean-spirited smile the moment she saw Mismis.

"How are you, Mismis? You're looking ever deplorable today."

"Oh, it's you, P. How have you been?"

"Who are you calling P?!"

Commander Pilie Commonsense was twenty-one, a year younger than Mismis, and she'd only recently been promoted. She came from a well-to-do family in the Empire and seemed as proper as any affluent girl should be. However, she had a major flaw. She was arrogant.

"I heard you barely squeak by at every bootcamp, Mismis."

Commander Pilie pushed up her glasses. She ran her gaze over the length of Mismis's body, taking the small commander in from the top of her head right to the tips of her toes.

"Goodness! You always give lackluster proposals during regular meetings and barely pass tests in any subject every time. And most of all, you look just like a little kid. You're a disgrace to the commanders."

"Hm. You think so?"

Commander Pilie was merciless in her verbal assault, but Mismis didn't react at all.

"But, P," she said.

"What is it?"

"Weren't you taken away on a stretcher just like me during last year's bootcamp?"

"Grk?!"

"And see, look at our heights. We're about the same size."

Indeed. Mismis only reached Iska's chest, and Commander Pilie was just about as petite. There was such little difference in their sizes, there was almost no point comparing them.

"Say, Iska," Nene quietly whispered into his ear as she compared the two girls. "Commander Pilie sure does pay a lot of attention to Commander Mismis."

"Yeah, I guess it's 'cause they're too similar, so she sees our commander as a rival."

As far as abilities went, Commander Pilie was nothing to write home about. She was below average in athleticism and terrible at shooting or operating machinery—Mismis was more or less the same in those areas.

The decisive difference was Pilie's elitism and her desire to climb the social ladder that came with it.

"Apparently, she puts in regular requests to get into the

promotion rack at the Imperial headquarters. She's famous for asking to be put into the running for management positions anytime an opening comes up," Jhin murmured. "She's in no position to laugh at the boss. Struggle all she might, she'll never get into HQ with those middling marks."

"Wh-who are you calling middling?!" Commander Pilie had turned around at Jhin's comment. "Sure, I'm not all that competent. That's true. But my grades are just barely below average. And Mismis is *way* below average. That makes a world of difference!"

"It really sounds the same, though..."

"It's different!" She briskly responded to Iska's comment. "Haah...I can't believe it. I have no clue why a Saint Disciple like Risya would ever associate with a failure of a commander like you."

"Well, we graduated the same year, so we're friends."

"That's exactly what I find unbelievable!" Commander Pilie pointed straight at Mismis. "Saint Disciples are the most honorable members of the forces and are selected by Their Excellency. Of course I wonder how someone like you is friendly with her."

"You're being so dramatic, P."

"Am I? You could easily use your friendship with a Saint Disciple to get a referral at the headquarters."

Then Pilie looked up at the ceiling and murmured, "I am so very jealous," before continuing. "No other woman has managed to climb up the career ladder like that. To be taught by her, the ideal elite soldier, is my dream!...Oh, Risya, please become my boss. And recommend me for the headquarters, too!"

Just then...the conference room door opened once again.

"Heeey, Mismis, how've you been?"

"Risya?!"

Pilie jumped up.

Risya In Empire—the tall commanding officer with intelligent and refined features—could have put even a model to shame. Though she was as young as Mismis, the talented woman had been promoted at an unprecedented speed until she was selected as a Saint Disciple, the top position in the Imperial Army.

"Mismis, Isk, Jhin-Jhin, and Nene. Yup, looks like we've got all four members of Unit 907 here…huh?" After she looked at Iska's unit, Risya shifted her gaze onto the fifth person in the room—the other commander. "Oh, is that you, P?"

"It's an honor to be in a mentor's presence, Risya, ma'am! You must have come here to see me!"

"No, not at all." She didn't beat around the bush. "Actually, I don't seem to remember ever becoming your mentor, P."

"What?! But don't you see how much I idolize you? I'm superior to Mismis as a commander in every way!"

"You're not doing a great job at hiding your ulterior motives." Risya stared coldly at Commander Pilie and let out a heavy sigh. "Besides, I know you're only flattering me in order to get a referral into headquarters."

"Grk?!"

"Now, let's compare your behavior to Mismis here!"

Mismis widened her eyes as Risya latched onto her from behind.

"She may be the textbook example of an incompetent commander, but she's got thick skin and sure is quiet. She's clumsy and sleeps in late, but that just makes her more like a difficult-to-manage pet!"

"Risya, that's not praise at all!"

"But it *is*. I'm trying to say you're as cute as a kitten."

"But you always tease me…"

"Only because your reactions are so adorable."

Mismis pouted, and Risya patted the commander's head. The

Saint Disciple actually did look as satisfied as an owner doting on her household pet.

"Oh, there was one more important thing I needed to tell you. Look at these, P."

"Look at what?"

"These, right here." Risya pointed at Mismis's chest, which ironically was quite mature compared to her baby face. "Isn't she amazing? Her breasts are so large that I can't even cover them with my hands! Her growth rate is second to none in that area."

"What's so wrong with being flat-chested?!" Commander Pilie turned bright red.

Commander Pilie's own bust happened to be very modest—a fact she was self-conscious of.

"Um…so, Ms. Risya? There's something we've been wondering about," Iska said.

"Hm? What's that, Isk?"

Iska had once been a Saint Disciple like Risya until a year ago, when he was demoted due to special reasons, so they were already acquainted with each other.

"You're very busy, aren't you, Ms. Risya? So why would you seek us out in our conference room?"

"Well, that's to make sure Mismis doesn't make a break for it when she hears about bootcamp. I need to keep a tight grip on her."

She was, in fact, holding Mismis right at that very moment. It seemed she wasn't just doting on the commander—she was restraining her, too.

"So, we've got Mismis secured."

"…Urgh. I thought it was suspicious that you swung by…"

"Ah-ha-ha! Serves you right, Mismis!" Commander Pilie shouted in joy when Mismis hung her head. "And the on-location cameras will capture just how you look as you struggle through bootcamp!"

"That goes for you too, P." Risya's single comment was enough to make Pilie freeze.

"What?"

"Twenty units are going to bootcamp at a time. Why do you think we've had you waiting on standby in the next conference room?"

"You can't mean that…"

"Your unit's going to bootcamp tomorrow, too."

"Noooooooo!"

"Well, have a nice trip to hell."

Risya dragged along both Mismis and Pilie. Meanwhile, Iska shared a look with Jhin and Nene as they watched the three leave them behind in the conference room.

———————

Bootcamp.

As the Imperial forces were in an ongoing war with the Paradise of Witches—also known as the Nebulis Sovereignty—bootcamp trained them for the variety of demanding situations that could present themselves during battle.

"Our enemies are not human. They are *monsters* called witches."

Imperial territory, east coast camp.

Twenty elite units had been gathered.

In front of a hundred Imperial soldiers, the supervising commander who was acting as the instructor shouted, "They share blood with the Grand Witch Nebulis, who once reduced the capital to ash. You will be going through training that will be indispensable in our fight against the witches."

"...Ahh. I remember last year's nightmare." Commander Mismis drooped over, despondent.

They had left the capital the night before and traveled a whole fourteen hours, rocked by a transport car the whole way. The unit hadn't slept or eaten in that time, but that was just another aspect of the training.

"I wanna go home already..."

"Oh, Mismis, you've already given up?" Next to her was the black-haired commander, Pilie. "I've already steeled myself for the worst. If you truly consider yourself a commander, you ought to be more prepared to set an example for your team."

"I can hear your voice quivering, P."

"Qu-quivering from excitement!"

"New recruits normally go through bootcamp for ten weeks."

The instructor kept his eyes trained on them. He was a middle-aged man who looked the very image of a military soldier, with an old, painful-looking scar across his face.

"But you are all professionals who have survived the battlefield numerous times. I have no worries that any of you will fail at this point, and I don't intend to prescreen any of you."

"Oh?" Mismis and Pilie both cocked their heads.

"Say, P, doesn't this sound perfect for us?"

"W-well, of course it does. We're already veterans."

"Yes, you should celebrate." The instructor's eyes glinted. "To ensure that none of you get bored, I've prepared a very *special* training regimen. I hope you all thoroughly enjoy the next seven days."

"Nooooooo!"

"That's completely unnecessary!"

The two commanders' shrieks echoed throughout the camp.

*   *   *

"…So? What do you think the instructor's planning on having us do in this wide-open space?"

They were in a sandy clearing. Jhin, who was in his combat uniform, was stretching to limber up.

"He said something about warming up first."

"I personally think we'll be running," Nene said. "Look, there are even white lines like for a marathon."

As Nene also stretched, she looked up at Iska.

"Iska? What do *you* think we're doing here?"

"I have no idea. I think it'd be too easy if we were just running, though…"

Iska had finished warming up earlier than everyone else.

All the other hundred plus soldiers were gathered at the grounds and doing their own exercises. The strain Iska saw on their faces was likely just his imagination.

"Whew…gotta stay calm. Gotta get through a week of this…"

"Commander Mismis, he's here."

The instructor had appeared at the clearing, just where Iska pointed.

He was holding a megaphone.

"Sorry to keep you waiting. Well, get into groups of two. Pair the tallest and shortest in your unit, then let the ones left over pair with each other."

"Groups of two, huh. We're a group of four, so looks like we'll split into two pairs." Commander Mismis turned to them.

The order from tallest to shortest within Unit 907 was as follows:

The sniper, Jhin.

Their vanguard (swordsman) Iska.

Their comms person Nene.

And Commander Mismis.

Since they were pairing the tallest and shortest in among themselves…

"Ugh…this is the worst. I have to be in a group with the boss? No way is this going to end well."

"Looks like I'm with you, Iska. Thank goodness!"

As Jhin sighed, Nene happily latched onto Iska. Meanwhile, behind them, Commander Mismis was shouting, "What's that supposed to mean?!"

"Mismis," Commander Pilie likewise shouted as she made a gallant appearance on the scene. "Hee-hee. This is a great opportunity."

"What is it, P?"

"I have a proposal. Trying to get through bootcamp is going to be a struggle, isn't it? So how about we make it more interesting—something like a game?" The black-haired commander pushed up her glasses. "We're probably forming groups to do relays. How about our pairs compete against each other?"

"…What?" Mismis openly scowled.

After all, when it came to athleticism, Mismis was the *least* capable in the Imperial forces. Even if Pilie was below average herself, Mismis would still be at a disadvantage in a competition.

"I'm terrible at running."

"That's why we're in pairs. You and your unit member have to work together to overcome your trials. That's the beauty of a team."

"So, Jhin?" Commander Mismis signaled at Jhin with her eyes. "You heard what P said. Do you think we can actually eke out a win?"

"Just let her do what she wants. But I think we've got exactly a fifty-fifty chance of winning. The stakes aren't bad."

"Oh, great job, Jhin...so, how'd you figure that out?"

"If I were alone, I'd have a hundred percent chance of victory. You'd have zero percent. The average of those two rates is fifty."

"Really, Jhin?!" Mismis exclaimed.

"Ah-ha-ha! You're so naive, Mismis! You think you have a fifty percent chance of victory?" Commander Pilie puffed out her chest and laughed loudly. "You should hold your tongue until you see my partner. Come, Bruno!"

"Hey."

His footsteps shook the ground with a *thud*.

A veritable giant stood behind the black-haired commander, towering at six and a half feet tall. The muscular new recruit who had appeared likely weighed in more than four hundred pounds.

"H-how is he one of your unit members?! P, you didn't have anyone like him before!"

"He's an up-and-coming rookie."

Next to him, Pilie looked like an actual child.

"I scouted him in order to make sure I'd get into headquarters."

"That's so unfair!"

"Part of being a commander is recruiting superior talent. And if I'm with Bruno, then this match is in the bag!"

The soldier was as big as a giant. Just looking up at him, he seemed like a mountain.

"Now, Instructor, tell us what we're doing!"

"Well, everyone, as a warm-up, we'll do a two-person marathon. It'll be three miles, and you'll be carrying some weight."

The announcement echoed throughout the grounds.

Commander Pilie nodded as though she'd been expecting it. "That's exactly what I was hoping for. With you around, Bruno, I'm sure we'll be able to carry a little extra baggage, easy—"

"You'll be carrying your partner."

"Huh?"

"The shorter one carries the taller one. And you'll run all the way through the woods."

Silence fell over the entire clearing. Common sense would have dictated that the larger person should carry the smaller one. So why were they doing the opposite?

"Oh, in other words, I'm supposed to carry you and run? Is that right?" Nene said to Iska. She pounded her fist against her other palm.

"Think you're up for it, Nene?"

"Of course! C'mon, get right on my back…Hee-hee. I can feel how warm you are."

"…Why'd you make that sound so creepy?!"

Nene seemed happy.

The issue was Jhin and Commander Mismis's pairing. To little surprise, Mismis's legs began to tremble the moment Jhin got on her back.

"Commander Mismis, are you okay?"

"I'm supposed to run like this?! There's no way I can do this for three miles. I couldn't even manage a hundred meters!"

"If you drop your partner before you finish, you start right over."

"What kind of rule is that?!"

The soldiers shrieked. This would undoubtedly be hard even for the brawniest men among them. As it so happened, the commander next to Mismis wailed the loudest of them all.

"That's absurd!"

Commander Pilie was a petite woman, and her partner was a giant man, so even picking him up would be a challenge.

"Urgh?! B-Bruno, you could stand to diet a little!"

"Sure, I'll look into it."

"Guh! J-just watch! Guuuuh!"

Pilie's face turned red as she lifted Bruno. Fittingly for a commander, she had the strength to pick up the several-hundred-pound giant.

Mismis stared at her with admiration.

"You're amazing, P!"

"O-of course I am…guh…running while carrying that light little unit member of yours wouldn't b-be true training for me…!"

"Then it's a race."

"What?"

"Just like you said, P. I'll carry Jhin and do my very best, too."

"Oh…well…about that."

Commander Pilie's legs were shaking from just the weight of her subordinate, but unfortunately for her, Mismis hadn't noticed.

"Uh, um, Mismis? Actually, I would like to call off the—"

"You may start."

"Let's go, Jhin!"

"No, waaaaaait!"

All the Imperial soldiers in the clearing began running at once. Mismis carried Jhin on her back. Nene carried Iska. Several dozen pairs took off for the forest up ahead.

And just one group was left behind.

"Y-you're too heavy! How is this supposed to be a warm-up?! I can't even run!"

"Commander, shouldn't we join everyone else?"

"You're too heavy for me to carry!"

As dust rose in the clearing, Commander Pilie's bellow of lament echoed all around.

Their goal was in the woods.

"*Wheeze wheeze, haah…haah*…three-mile marathon, my butt…!"

Commander Pilie leaned against a tree, sweat coating her entire body. Naturally, she was in last place.

"That damn instructor. I can't believe he changed the goal just before we got to the finish line. We had to run another half a mile—there's such a thing as taking it too far when toying with people's emotions, you know."

"Hee-hee. This is my first time winning against you in a competition, P!" Next to her, Mismis was in high spirits.

"Not much of a win when you're second from last," Jhin quipped.

"Oh, Jhin, don't say that. All you had to do was hang out while on my back," Mismis said, though she still seemed to be brimming with energy. Since Pilie had taken so long to finish, everyone else had ended up having quite a long break, Mismis and Nene included.

"…I-it wasn't supposed to be like this."

"Are you okay, P?"

"S-spare me the pity! The terms of the race were just unfair, is all. You can't really believe you won simply because of that." Commander Pilie gnashed her teeth. "The next exercise will be the real competition. Bootcamp is just getting started!"

"Good work, you all!"

The instructor's announcement echoed throughout the woods. His calm voice was the polar opposite of Pilie's heated tone.

"There's another six miles to camp. You'll go *straight through the forest*—but be warned—wild beasts make frequent appearances around here."

"So this is a scenario that assumes we might go through guerilla warfare in a jungle. Excellent."

Pilie had a rifle in her hand. Beside her, Mismis held a handgun.

"Beasts...what should we do, P? What if we run into a lion?"

"There aren't lions in the jungle, Mismis. You should be more concerned about wild bears."

The twenty units headed deeper into the woods. Mismis and Pilie, as the commanders, led the way through the vegetation as Iska, Nene, and Jhin guarded them from behind.

"Say, Iska, considering how evil bootcamp is, they've probably set up traps around here. We should warn Commander Mismis to be careful."

"Yeah, we probably should just in case."

They ran up to Mismis's side.

"How's it going, Commander? The rest of us have been keeping an eye out, but if you spot anything suspicious, let us know."

"I haven't seen anything...but what do you think of that?"

Mismis stopped in her tracks.

Commander Pilie, who also stood next to her, was exchanging worried glances with her subordinates.

"P, what do you think?"

"Don't ask me. It's not like we can march through this bottomless muddy swamp."

Yes. A murky black swamp spread before them, blocking their way.

"I'm not sure I'd say it's bottomless, but it does look pretty deep."

Commander Pilie tried lowering a stick into the water to check its depth, but she didn't reach the bottom.

"It must go up to my stomach...or maybe even deeper. We should probably go around it," Pilie called out loud enough for the unit behind her to hear, "Everyone, we need to backtrack about ten meters. Let's head farther right from the animal trail from earlier!"

"Commander Mismis, Commander Pilie, you've misunderstood the assignment."

"......Come again?"

At that moment, they heard a stern voice address them. The instructor had sent a simultaneous transmission through all of the comms they'd brought with them.

"I said to forge straight ahead."

"...Which means?"

"Use your head. You're moving forward through a jungle. The witch forces are closing in from both sides and behind you. Do you think you can afford to waste time retreating while surrounded?"

"You can't possibly mean..." Commander Pilie audibly gulped from nerves.

"You charge forward *into* the swamp."

"I knew it!"

Pilie eyed the pitch-black murk. Upon closer inspection, tiny bugs were floating around in it. If mosquito larvae were living in the water, they could bet full-grown ones would be around too—along with tons of other microorganisms.

If any of them had open wounds, they would end up with parasites. "I'll head in first. Commander Mismis, you come in after me."

"Iska, a-are you sure you'll be okay?!"

He walked forward and immediately stepped into the swamp.

Dwoosh...

The tip of his shoe sunk in. Once he was chest-deep in the water, he finally reached the bottommost part of the swamp.

"Y-you're okay?"

"Luckily my feet can reach the bottom. But I think it'd reach up to your neck."

The smell and the slime permeated into his clothes. It was utterly revolting. It'd soaked through every layer of his clothing, from his combat uniform all the way to his undergarments.

"Commander Mismis, you come in slowly."

"Ye...yes. Ah! This is the worst. It splashed into my mouth...!" Mismis scowled.

Jhin and Nene followed. The units watching behind them steeled themselves as they stepped into the swamp as well.

There was a single female commander among them who hadn't moved, however. She only stared at the swamp with a frown.

"P, hurry up and get in."

"I—I know...!"

Commander Pilie was pale as she extended her leg. She let out a small yelp the moment her foot met the water.

"Ugh! Out of all the things we had to do, why did it have to be my worst nightmare..."

Shoulder-deep in the swamp, she started walking, her face tense.

Commander Pilie headed to Mismis's side.

"P, you don't look so good."

"Anyone who's okay with this would have to be off their rockers. Ugh...the swamp water is getting on my face, and I see these fuzzy bugs wriggling right in front of my eyes. And the goop is even inside my clothes."

She hesitantly continued into the swamp.

Had they been in the clear water of an ocean or river, they would have been able to see the bottom, but as it was, they had no idea what lurked beneath.

Nene and Iska murmured to each other.

"Iska, do you think there might be alligators hiding in here?"

"They live in fresh water, so maybe. We should keep an eye on the surface. Check for any suspicious bubbles."

"A-alligators?!" As she overheard their conversation, Commander Pilie flinched. "Ugh, how far does this swamp go? For someone raised with my pedigree, this is the least fitting training I could possibly think of…!"

"P, watch out ahead of you."

"What?"

"A snake's swimming in front of you, so be careful."

"…"

Pilie's pupils constricted. The water was up to her shoulders, so she was eye-level with the snake. She stared into its eyes,

"Ahhhhhhhh?!" The loudest scream they'd heard yet echoed deep into the woods.

"P-please help me, Mismis!"

"It already slithered away."

"What?"

Pilie latched onto Mismis's arm and blinked, wide-eyed.

"Looks like your scream scared it off."

"Th-that wasn't a scream just now. Uh, um…I was warning my subordinates of the danger, that's what I was doing! Actually, Mismis, how are you okay right now?!"

"What do you mean?"

"I—I mean, this is a smelly and unsanitary *swamp*. The snake was right in front of your eyes."

"Was it?"

"It was!"

"I'd be afraid of a venomous one, but I don't mind animals."

Mismis kept plowing forward through the swamp. As she led

the large group, she seemed gallant and reassuring even to Iska and the other subordinates.

"...But it's a swamp. You're not grossed out?"

"I used to play in the mud all the time as a kid. This training might not be so bad, actually."

"Wh-what?!" Pilie was speechless for a moment. "Are you saying you're enjoying this?"

"I don't like it, but it's better than running or swimming or anything that requires being more active, don't you think?"

"Y-you think this is *easy*?!" Commander Pilie widened her eyes in shock.

Only now did she realized how Mismis had become an Imperial commander. She was far below average when it came to physical abilities, especially of anyone in the Imperial forces. However, what this exercise required wasn't a body of steel, but a *heart* of steel. Thick skin, in other words.

Even the brawniest of soldiers could have a mental breakdown. But someone who could forge ahead in harsh conditions, through mud and muck, would have the force of will needed to endure the agony of war. That was what Mismis had.

"Right...I can't imagine Mismis being put off by swarms of insects or a little mud..."

Mismis headed deeper into the swamp. There was a large group of men far bigger than her, yet they seemed to naturally follow behind her.

Let's go where's she's heading.

Commander Pilie shuddered at the situation.

"N-no, I can't accept this...I can't allow myself to be defeated by another commander, even at bootcamp!"

Mismis didn't even mind the swamp water splashing on her.

As she parted through the water to lead them, the others followed behind...until someone passed her.

"Heh-heh. What do you think now, Mismis? Look, I've taken the lead in the blink of an eye!"

"Hang on, Commander Pilie," Iska called out to her as she forged farther and farther ahead. "I need to tell you something."

"Oh, aren't you one of Mismis's men? What is it?" Pilie wore a victorious grin. "Have you figured out what makes the difference between me and Mismis? It's merciless, but the Imperial forces is a dog-eat-dog world. Only the best can work at headquarters. And it is I who—"

"You've got a leech on your back."

"Excuse me?"

A leech—a type of slug that lives in swamps and sucks human blood. And one was stuck right on her back.

"P...!" Seeing that, Mismis gave her a compassionate look. "Did you take the lead because you knew there were leeches in this swamp? You were protecting me, weren't you?!"

"W-wait a sec?!"

The commander squirmed in panic, but the leech wasn't coming off.

"Take it off! Your name's Iska, right? Take this thing off me immediately!"

"Got it. There's no need to panic."

"I hate leeeeeches!"

She teared up as she made her pitiful confession.

———

It was night in the jungle.

Twenty tents were set up at the Imperial camp.

Snap, snap…

They'd started an open fire to ward off beasts and sprayed themselves with bug repellant before turning in.

They were still wearing the same clothes from when they'd gone through the swamp.

"Ahh. My clothes are still only half dry. This feels so gross. And there's still mud in my ponytail…"

After finishing the rations, which could hardly be called palatable, Nene drooped her shoulders in disappointment.

Lights out was at eight.

At this time of night, the Imperial capital's business district would have been in full swing, but they were in a jungle far from the city center. Once eight rolled around, the entire area was enveloped in darkness.

"Iska, we're waking up at three in the morning, right?"

"That's what we were told. It's a little early, but pretty standard for bootcamp. Whether we can actually sleep is a separate matter," Iska replied, his clothes covered in mud as well.

Even if they were training under the assumption it was for a long battle, the unpleasant feeling of the clothes against their skin still affected them. Their extensive military experience couldn't change that fact.

"Ahh. I can't believe we're covered in mud right from day one. I'm so disappointed," Nene said.

She scowled as she looked down at her clothes.

"I was so excited to stay in a tent with Iska again after so long. But considering how muddy we are, there's probably not much of a chance of anything exciting happening with you at night."

"What were you even expecting?!"

He averted his gaze from Nene's somewhat suspicious puppy-dog eyes.

"Jhin, say something, please."

"Don't pay her attention. She's just spouting nonsense," Jhin responded bluntly and lay down in the back of the tent. "It's been a while since we've camped out, and you're all making it seem like a school field trip. Hey, Nene, leave the lookout to the squad and let's all get some sleep."

"What…? But…"

Nene looked unhappy.

"I'm not sleepy yet. And my clothes feel gross since they're still half wet."

"Just close your eyes and hunker down. We've still got a long way to—" Jhin stopped midsentence.

"Exactly!" Suddenly, a figure appeared at the entrance to their unit's tent. "Hello, Mismis. I had an unexpected and embarrassing defeat today, but this is when the real bootcamp starts!"

Commander Pilie had come by in her mud-covered combat uniform. Afternoon training had evidently taken a toll on her. Her face was still pale.

"We'll settle this tomorrow!…Wait, Mismis?"

"She's already asleep."

Iska pointed at the center of the tent. Commander Mismis was already curled up in her sleeping bag, deep asleep. She showed no sign of waking, despite the fact that Pilie had shouted her name at the top of her lungs.

"She won't wake up until morning. Actually, she'll probably sleep until afternoon if we don't wake her up."

"How shameless can she be?!"

Pilie had also spotted the ration containers that Mismis had eaten from. The rations were meant to stay edible as long as possible, so they tasted terrible. Even soldiers in peak physical condition hadn't been able to find it within themselves to finish them.

Mismis, on the other hand, had eaten everything. Her stomach was far from ordinary.

"...I had to give up halfway through."

"The commander seemed to enjoy the food. She doesn't quibble about how things taste."

"What kind of palate does she have?!"

Pilie backed away without thinking.

"Well...I suppose I should reevaluate my impression of you, Mismis."

She'd finished off the rations that broke even the most robust of men, and she was unfazed by the harsh sleeping conditions.

Pilie once again realized Mismis truly had an iron will. Her physical abilities were obviously lacking, but she had a useful military skill worthy of special mention, even if it wasn't measurable by standard means.

"I underestimated you...So this is why Risya has taken a shine to you. It seems you have some talents, then."

"No, I think Ms. Risya just likes how Commander Mismis looks."

"No, I know I'm right about this!" Pilie clenched her fist and yelled. "I understand now. Mismis was my actual archrival all along. That's my path to becoming an elite member of the forces and finding a way into headquarters—defeating my greatest rival!"

"You think so?"

"I doubt it," Nene said.

"You're overestimating her. The boss isn't that special."

Despite their remarks, Commander Pilie already had her mind made up and simply wouldn't listen—she was too wrapped up in herself to realize it.

"But I won't lose to her. You better be prepared, Mismis! Let's give it our all tomorrow!" she declared, then turned around, seeming satisfied with herself. "Good day, Mismis. I'll see you in the morning!"

"She didn't hear any of that because she's sleeping, though…"

Pilie briskly walked away.

As the commander continued to snooze, Iska, Jhin, and Nene shared looks.

"Seems like a huge boon to Commander Mismis for her reputation to improve just from sleeping…"

"I'm a little jealous."

"Just leave her alone. We've got to go to bed soon, too."

Morning arrived.

"Hello, everyone."

The instructor nodded in satisfaction after he inspected the line of one hundred soldiers.

"Had you been new recruits, some of you would have failed last night. I expect nothing less from a group with a long history of service. I'm glad to see you're well rested."

"Hmph…He sounds so insincere. It's shameless, right, Iska?" Nene rubbed her eyes sleepily. "If he actually wanted to let us get a decent night's sleep, he would've let us take a shower. And I wish he'd let us change out of these muddy clothes."

"It's just one of those things they say during training."

"I know, but still…" Nene crossed her arms, still displeased.

On the other hand, Mismis, who'd slept very well, was in tip-top shape.

"Huh? P, you've got dark circles under your eyes."

"Grk?!"

"Did you not sleep well yesterday? Are you okay?"

"...I can't understand how anyone could be so insensitive that they could sleep through that evening. But your concern is unnecessary!" Pilie stared at Mismis with her tired, bloodshot eyes, and ground her molars. "This bootcamp isn't enough to frighten me. Why, even yesterday I was so bored, I was yawning!"

"...Oh?"

"What? Instructor?!"

He had appeared before Pilie's eyes. The veteran military soldier squinted in delight when he heard her audacious remarks.

"That's the spirit, Commander Pilie. So, the training I had carefully planned out is a yawnfest to you, is it? It's been a while since I've heard a woman such as yourself say something with so much backbone."

"Ah-wah...n-no, I didn't mean that. I was just riling Mismis up..."

"It sounded more like a passionate declaration of love to me. Don't worry. I've prepared a most *stimulating* set of exercises for the remaining six days."

"Nooooo!"

On the second day of bootcamp, Commander Pilie's wails resounded once more at who knows what time that day.

"All right, everyone, put these cuffs on your wrists and legs."

Everyone was immobilized before they were tied to the back of a large car and dragged along a gravel road. This drill was supposed to prepare them for a scenario where they were captured by witches.

"Ow, ow ow ow ow! C-come on! This should be enough. Please stop the car! I'm getting friction burns!"

As she was dragged to the other side of the grounds by the vehicle, Commander Pilie disappeared in a cloud of dust.

Eventually, even her shrieks died away.

"Whoa…!"

As Mismis watched the ghastly scene, she scrunched up her face, and even the brawny male soldiers standing behind her recoiled.

"I-Iska, doesn't this seem even more physically demanding than yesterday's training?"

"Men get dragged two hundred meters, while women get dragged a hundred meters."

"It looks like P is being dragged four hundred meters, though?"

"I guess that's the instructor's way of showing his affection for her…"

They wouldn't necessarily be spared a similar experience. The tradition at bootcamp was for each passing day to become more brutal.

"Just six more days to get through, Commander."

"…Right."

"Let's go to your favorite barbecue place after this is over."

"…Okay."

Commander Mismis, however, had already turned pale as a ghost.

———————————

Finally, the seventh day of bootcamp arrived.

It was the last morning they would be there. The soldiers, who had finished their training, were currently gathered deep in the jungle under a precipitous cliff.

Or rather, they weren't soldiers so much as corpses lying on the ground.

"I can't do it anymore…I can't eat one more bite of those gross rations," Nene said. "I want to get back to the capital and have a decent meal as soon as we can…"

"C'mon, get off the ground, Nene. Iska, how's the situation over there?"

"The commander collapsed and isn't moving."

Jhin helped Nene to her feet. Beyond them, Iska was trying to talk to Mismis, who was lying facedown.

"Come on, Commander."

"I'm at my limit…"

"Don't say that. Look, we need to line up now. And the helicopter should be coming to get us soon, too."

Soldiers were transported back to the capital using a helicopter after training was over. All they had to do now was wait for it.

"Great job getting through the weeklong bootcamp, everyone."

The instructor's voice boomed. He was addressing them through speakers, so he wasn't anywhere to be seen.

"The helicopter will be arriving shortly. One of the higher-ups will be on the copter, and I'm sure she'll express her appreciation for you going through such rigorous training."

"I-it's finally over!" Commander Pilie, who was pale and burnt-out, rose shakily to her feet. "Now we just go home on the helicopter…ah, a warm meal and a bed…then I'll take a bath and be free of this mud."

"However…"

"However…?"

"I have an unfortunate announcement for you all. The landing location of the helicopter has been changed. It is no longer coming to the bottom of the cliff."

"…Come again?"

Pilie and Mismis's smiles froze.

"It will be arriving at the top of the cliff in front of you."

"On *top* of it?!"

Pilie paled as she looked upward.

It was steep, and twenty meters tall. And of course there wasn't a single rope or ladder around to help them climb up.

"It couldn't be......"

"Use your bare hands to climb up the cliff. This is your last exercise for bootcamp."

"Y-you've got to be kidding! We're already on our last legs!"

"The helicopter will only stay here for one hour. Anyone who doesn't make it in time will be left behind."

At the bottom of the cliff, the soldiers' wails tore through area. Their final trial had begun.

"This is terrible! No one said anything about a final exercise!" Commander Mismis lamented as she desperately groped at the rough rockface. "So if we don't climb this cliff, we're going to be stuck here?!"

"Hey, Boss, you better not slip!"

"I—I know!" Mismis nervously nodded at Jhin, who was right below her.

It had rained last night, so the rockface was slippery. They weren't simply at their physical limit. If they weren't straining their already fully worn nerves, they'd lose their grip and fall.

"If you fall even once, we'll have to climb back up, and we won't get there in time."

"Ye...yes. Iska, Nene, how are you doing?!" Mismis asked.

"I think I'll manage. How are you, Iska?"

"I'm fine. Commander Mismis, this area of the cliff has a lot of divots, so it's going to be easier to climb."

Iska scaled the rock above them. Mismis was behind him, then Nene, then Jhin. However...

The instructor had added a stipulation that the entire unit had to be tied together by rope. If one person slipped, then everyone would fall. What a malicious rule.

"W-wait a sec, Iska. I'm terrible at this..."

"Commander Mismis, raise your right foot next. And reach for that crevice over there."

"I'm not sure I can reach..."

Climbing was no easy task for Mismis since she was so short. Commander Pilie's unit followed right after them.

"This is our final showdown, Mismis. C'mon, everyone. Almost there. We need to pass Unit 907 while Mismis is struggling...let's get to the top of the cliff quickly now!"

As Pilie grew impatient, her fingers slipped.

"Oh..."

"Careful, P!"

She started to fall, before someone caught her in just the nick of time—not one of her subordinates, but Mismis herself.

"Are you okay?"

"Y-you..." Pilie stared at Mismis as though she couldn't believe it. "Wh-why did you catch me...? Your entire unit would have fallen if you fell trying to help me!"

They were all exhausted from the seven days of bootcamp, and Mismis must have reached her limit, too. So then why?

"What? Well, you're my friend."

"...Huh?!"

Friend.

That word left Pilie speechless. She'd thought Mismis would rattle off a canned explanation about them being fellow members of the Imperial forces or something.

"You're saying we're *friends*…?"

"Aren't we?"

"You're just so…"

"What?" Commander Mismis gave her an innocent look. Pilie had been sure she hated the other woman, yet Mismis's eyes were so dazzling in the moment that she couldn't bear to look at her fellow commander.

"…Pfft!"

"P?"

"I'll admit it, then. Commander Mismis Klass, you've bested me."

She tightened her grip on the hand that held hers. For the first time in her life, and with a fresh-faced smile, Pilie had acknowledged her own defeat.

"I'll admit that you've won—just today."

The final training.

The hundred soldiers used their last bit of strength to climb up the cliff to the helicopter waiting for them at the top. The instructors and higher-ups of the Empire were there waiting for them. A special guest had come to greet them with a warm reception after they'd endured the brutalities of the bootcamp.

"Yoo-hoo, everyone. How are you all?"

"Huh? Risya?!" Mismis's eyes went wide.

Risya, the Saint Disciple, had appeared from out of the helicopter. "Mm-hmm. Looks like you're all worse for wear. But you did a great job."

"Risya?!" Pilie shouted.

Just then, she scaled the cliff and came over to Risya at breakneck speed.

"You came! Please take a look! I did such a wonderful job!"

Tears began to form in her eyes. She flung out her arms for a hug.

"Please! Please refer me to headquarters this time!"

"Aw, you sure did work hard."

"My dear mentor!"

Risya opened her arms welcomingly, so Pilie ran forward…

"Good job, Mismis!"

"…Huh?"

…only to pass right by Risya. The Saint Disciple had ignored what should have been her moving embrace with Pilie in order to latch onto Mismis.

"Uh. What?" Commander Pilie watched them in shock from the sidelines.

"Were you doing all right, Mismis? Mm-hmm, you're so cute when you're tired."

"C'mon, Risya. I'm too exhausted for this right now."

"So what? You're so cute when you're disgruntled, too."

Risya started to tousle Mismis's hair.

She never acted that way with anyone else, yet here she was, lovingly doting on Mismis.

"This is an important method of bonding. Since we're both fellow Imperial force members," Risya said.

"Personally, I think you're just teasing me."

"Ah-ha-ha. Was it that obvious?"

Pilie watched the whole scene unfold.

"…"

The black-haired commander balled her hands into tight fists as she began to tremble.

"L-listen up, Risya…and also Mismis."

No one was listening, however.

Risya was too occupied with Mismis, who was doing her best to fight off the superior officer.

"Please stop, Risya!"

"Hm. Oh, just let me."

"..."

And...

"I—I don't feel humiliated at all, I'll have you know!" Pilie was shouting herself hoarse. "Mismis! You're my archnemesis! Remember that!"

Then she ran off at full speed.

From that point on, Commander Pilie's rivalry with Mismis intensified, but that story is for another time.

———

Meanwhile, in a land far, far away from the Empire...

In the Paradise of Witches, at the Nebulis Sovereignty's palace...

"Lady Alice, I have a report for you."

"Oh, what is it, Rin?"

When her dear attendant addressed her, the girl turned around. Aliceliese Lou Nebulis IX.

She was a princess with brilliant golden locks and a charming face.

She and the Imperial swordsman Iska had acknowledged each other as rivals, but only the two of them shared that secret.

"What is the report, then?"

"It concerns the east coast base within the Imperials' territory. We've received intelligence that a camp has been set up there."

"Do you suppose it's for a military drill?"

"Yes. It seems that several of their main units are participating. I believe it would be wise to have the astral corps look into what they are doing."

"I'll leave that decision to those on the scene, then."

She sighed.

For some reason, Alice felt disappointed after hearing the report. She was, in fact, truly disappointed. She hadn't been hoping for information about the Imperial camp.

"That's not it," she said. "I don't need to know about the trainings. What I want to know is where Iska is being dispatched to. I want to know which battlefield he'll be at."

"Lady Alice...that again?"

The attendant's shoulders drooped when she saw her lady's behavior.

Alice had been like this all the time lately. She only thought about when she would be able to fight her enemy—the Imperial swordsman Iska. Everything else had become an afterthought.

"You never know. The swordsman might be at the training camp."

"That would be too much of a coincidence." Alice answered her attendant's joke as she stared out the window...

Toward the enemy nation...

Toward the Imperial territories.

"I want to finally settle things between the two of us. Just where in the world could Iska be?"

File 03

Our Last Crusade or
Life in a Flower Garden of Women

Our Last **CRUSADE** OR THE RISE OF A *New World*
Secret File

CONFIDENTIAL

"Iska, I think I'll stay in your room starting today."

"……Come again?"

"It'll be fine—rest assured I'll bring my own change of clothes and toothbrush and cup. Yay! I'm so looking forward to this!"

"What's happening here?!"

And that was how Iska's holiday started, first thing in the morning, when Nene made her announcement.

The war between the two world superpowers…

The Empire that Iska and his companions were part of were in an ongoing, century-long conflict with the Paradise of Witches, the Nebulis Sovereignty.

And this was a regular day in the life of the Imperial forces.

"Ah! Hey, Iska, did you hear about that thing?"

"What thing?"

Nene ran over to Iska as he walked through the military base. She was a charming soldier with a slim figure who wore her red hair in a ponytail.

"You know! The base expansion plan. They're remodeling the barracks we live in."

"Of course I've heard. What about it?"

"It's awful! They're renovating the women's barracks first, but they're going to replace all the walls and floors with this new flame-resistant material, so we're all being thrown out of our rooms." She sighed and her shoulders drooped. "They told all the soldiers that we need to pack up our things and find somewhere else to live during construction. So there's been a huge uproar about it."

"That came from headquarters, didn't it? I got the notice, too."

Iska wasn't entirely unaffected. Once the women's barracks were done, they'd do the men's, so he was in the middle of cleaning up his room.

"But I heard the compensation isn't bad. You can stay at an Imperial hotel during that time."

"Yeah, that's true, but…," Nene said hesitantly. For some reason, her face was red as she gave him a pleading look. "Iska, I think I'll stay in your room starting today."

"……Come again?" He doubted he heard her correctly. The conversation was moving so quickly that he had no idea how to even respond.

"It'll be fine—rest assured, I'll bring my own change of clothes and toothbrush and cup. Yay! I'm so looking forward to this!"

"Wait! What's happening?! None of this is making any sense!"

Headquarters was covering the cost of staying in hotel rooms while the women's barracks were being renovated. Nene shouldn't have had any issues.

"Why my room? You're a girl… It's going to be hard to sneak you into the men's barracks."

"I don't mind," Nene said.

"But other people will! And my room isn't that big in the first place, so it'll be a hundred times better for you at a hotel."

"So, about that..." Nene looked around. Apparently the next part was something she couldn't have others hearing. "I just got the hotel stipend. From headquarters."

"It's a lot, isn't it? I heard they pay for a week of hotel expenses and food."

Living in a hotel wasn't cheap. They wouldn't be able to use the dining hall at the barracks, so they'd likely have to eat at the expensive restaurant within the hotel, hence why headquarters was giving them the money for those expenses. They shouldn't have any trouble at all.

"That's why I want to stay in your room."

"Like I said, I don't understand!"

She was being compensated for the hotel expenses. So why was Nene hounding him about staying in his room?

"Nene, explain."

"Basically, while we're out of the barracks, we need to live off of the stipend, but we don't have to return the leftover money. Which means..."

"Yes?"

"If I stay in your room, then I'd be able to save on hotel costs. Then the stipend would be for me to spend however I want!"

"That's underhanded!"

"No, it's not!" Nene proudly thrust out her chest. "Other women are staying at their friend's places or with relatives, too. We all want to use that money for ourselves or to go on trips."

"...Wow, they're invested."

Though they'd been given a stipend, they hadn't been told where to stay.

That's basically what Nene was saying. It was just clever enough that headquarters would probably let it slide. The ingenuity of the female soldiers was nothing to scoff at.

"But the men's barracks is…"

"They won't find me in your room. And we stayed in the same tent during training. There shouldn't be any issues."

"So that's your reasoning, then…"

Iska and Nene were part of the same unit, so they'd stayed in the same tent before.

"Please?" Nene pleaded, looking up at him with her adorable puppy-dog eyes.

They both stared at each other in silence.

Iska was the first one to break it.

"…All right, I give in. Just this once."

"Yay! Thank you, Iska! I'll bring my stuff right away!"

After leaping in joy, Nene took off down the hall.

Commander Mismis, his superior, appeared afterward.

"Ah! There you are, Iska."

Though she was short and only reached up to Iska's chest, she was actually a full-grown adult. She was also an Imperial commander having experienced many battles.

"Nene and I won't be able to live in our rooms because of the construction. Did you know we'll need to live in a hotel for a week?"

"Right…"

"Let me stay in your room?"

"You can't be serious?! What are you saying, Commander? You could enjoy staying at a hotel!"

He immediately questioned her, but she wasn't backing down.

"This is an order from your superior officer. Starting today, your room will be Unit 907's base of operations."

"What kind of order is that?!…All right, I'll bite. Why are you doing this?"

"Well, a hotel wouldn't be on the base," Commander Mismis breezily replied. "Even the closest one would force us to walk from the business district. I don't think that'd be any good, now would it?"

Beyond the window, Commander Mismis pointed in the direction of the business district.

"As part of Special Division III, we're supposed to be emergency personnel. Our role is to gather faster than anyone else if the war against the Nebulis Sovereignty expands in scope. In which case, as Imperial force members, we should stay in your room rather than in a far-off hotel!"

"What?!"

He sure hadn't thought of that. Out of all the ridiculous things he could have imagined Mismis saying, Iska never would have expected her to go for that angle.

"I'm so impressed, Commander Mismis! I was convinced that you'd say you just wanted to keep the hotel money like Nene..."

"Well, there's that, too."

"What?! Then you really are just in it for the money!"

"Hang on, Iska!" Commander Mismis held out her hand, forcing him to stop. "Not so fast. Just like I told you, my goal is respectable and strategic. Getting the hotel money to spend for myself is just a bonus."

"Then you can stay in my room, but will you give back the hotel money to headquarters?"

"No way."

"Then you really are after the money!"

"Come on, Iska, what's wrong with that?"

Then the commander took his hand and started walking to the men's barracks.

"Nene's staying in your room already anyway."

"How did you find that out?!"

Now Iska was flustered. Though Nene and Mismis were in the same unit as he was, he'd have a huge problem on his hands if anyone found out there were women in his room. The whole thing was supposed to have been between him and Nene.

"Nene told me."

"Nene!"

"Say, Iska, you wouldn't invite Nene to your room but not your own commander, would you?"

Mismis wore a confident smile that said she wouldn't take any arguments as she slowly drew closer to him.

"Or do you mean you two have *that* kind of relationship?"

"We don't!"

"All right, then. It's settled!"

"......Fine."

An hour later...

Commander Mismis and Nene showed up to Iska's room, large travel bags in tow.

"Yay! It's been a while since I've been in your room, Iska."

"I've visited a few times, but this is my first time staying the night."

They were sleeping over at the men's barracks. The unusual state of affairs had made the two women excited—they were almost treating this like a school trip.

"Let's see. As a commander, I should also check in on my subordinates' private lives. Let me see the inside of your fridge first... Wow, looks like you even cook for yourself."

"Commander, let's check his bed, too."

"Nene, we save the best for last. Let's start with the bath."

"What are you two doing?!"

They opened the fridge and closet, then systematically

inspected the books on his shelf. They both even headed to his bathroom together, their eyes gleaming as they looked around.

"Hmm, your reaction seems...," Nene started to say.

"Suspicious," Mismis finished for her. "He seems fishy, Nene. He must be hiding something."

"You two are the shady ones here! Why are you combing through my room like you're spies?!"

Iska wasn't worried about anything they'd find—or he wanted to believe he wasn't. Then again, with two women searching his place this thoroughly, he couldn't help but feel nervous.

"...Would you like some tea? You two can rest in the living room."

"Okaaay!"

"Sounds great. I'll make myself at home."

The two of them flopped down onto the living room floor.

"Um..."

"What is it, Iska?"

"Oh, nothing, Commander. You just settle in, then..."

He had told them to relax, but he hadn't told them to lie down. He even almost started to comment on it but managed to stop himself. He had a bad feeling about this. Was this even his room anymore?

"Oh...right, I wanted to ask you two—why my room? You could have picked Jhin's. He also lives in the men's barracks."

Unit 907 consisted of four members. There was Commander Mismis, Nene who was in charge of their communications, and Iska. The final member was Jhin, their sniper, but the two women didn't seem to have any intention of imposing on him.

"......Hm. You know how it is, right, Nene?"

"Yeah, Jhin can be a bit...," she trailed off. The two shared a look.

"Well, I mean, Jhin is super particular. Everything was so clean when I went over to his place. I was shocked. There wasn't a speck of dust around."

"That's right. His room is even cleaner than most of the girls' rooms. It'd be a little, well, stressful, for us to live there, right?" Nene lounged on the floor as she said this. "We prefer your room. Considering the state of yours, unlike Jhin, you probably wouldn't get mad at us if we didn't clean for three days. Right, Commander?"

"That's right. I think you wouldn't mind if we got your room a little messy." Commander Mismis was also lying about on the floor next to Nene. "I bet you'd be okay if we accidentally knocked beer cans over or spilled stuff on the floor. We could probably leave crumbs around, too."

"No way would I be okay with that!"

"Then what about leaving our pajamas on the ground?"

"That would be embarrassing for you, so please don't!"

Even if Mismis was his superior officer, this was still Iska's room. This was his home—his guests ought to be abiding by his rules.

"Look, you two. While you're staying with me, you need to have some self-control—"

Ker-chak.

Just at that moment, the locked door was forced open from outside.

"Heeey! Mismis, Nene, Isk. Been a while since I saw you three."

"Ms. Risya?!"

"Don't mind me."

A giant suitcase thudded down at the entryway when Risya—a bespectacled woman and one of the military's higher-ups—sauntered into the room as though it were her own.

She was the Lord's staff officer. Though she should have been far out of their reach since she was in the upper echelons of the military, she'd been friends with Mismis since they'd attended military school together.

"Oh, Isk. I'll have tea too, please. Three teaspoons of milk with three grams of sugar. And ninety degrees would be great, but I won't quibble."

"Make it yourself!"

"Oh, what trouble I'm in. Aren't you curious about why I've come all the way here?"

"..." Iska flicked his eyes toward suitcase Risya had brought with her. He had a bad feeling about this.

It seemed like she was there for the same reason as Commander Mismis and Nene.

"I'm not curious at all. So please don't explain and go straight home."

"Were you aware the women's barracks are under construction?"

"...I'd really rather not know."

"Now, now, Isk. Weren't you once a fellow Saint Disciple? Won't you let me rant about work?"

Risya made herself at home sitting cross-legged right on the floor. After seeing that, Commander Mismis suddenly got up.

"Huh? But you're one of the higher-ups, Risya. You don't live in the women's barracks, do you? You shouldn't have been driven out."

"I *shouldn't* have, but the construction noise is just so loud."

Risya sipped at the tea Iska had poured her. He hadn't actually checked the temperature of the tea or added milk or sugar, but she didn't seem to mind.

"I'm in management, so I don't live in the barracks, but the noise was so loud that I couldn't sleep yesterday. My skin has been terrible, and the stress is really getting to me. Say, Isk, do you have any snacks to go with this tea? Maybe some cookies?"

"This isn't a café, you know!"

"Anyway, I don't live in the barracks, which means they won't give me a hotel stipend. I'd need to pay my own way...but then I came up with a solution!" Risya pointed at the suitcase. "I could stay with Mismis at the hotel she was in! But then she told me she would be in your room, Isk."

"There's no way."

"I haven't even said anything yet."

"You basically have, though!"

He knew Risya had to have packed everything she needed for an overnight stay into that suitcase.

"My room is cramped enough already with Commander Mismis and Nene here."

"You're fine with it, right, Mismis?"

"Sure."

"What about my opinion? You should value the opinions of your subordinates, too!"

"My subordinates, huh. Nene, what do you think?"

"It's fine."

"But what about *mine*?!"

It was three against one.

After the three women had invaded his room like a storm, Iska found his personal space under military occupation.

———

Thus, a girls gathering commenced during the sleepover.

"Living in Iska's room is a little dreary now that I'm here." Commander Mismis looked around the sunlit room.

It was a studio. The living room was somewhat spacious, but because it also contained Iska's bed, bookshelf, and other furniture, it felt more cramped.

"Well, it *is* the men's barracks."

"That's not what I mean. Iska, this place isn't decorative enough!" Commander Mismis said as she got up. Or rather, she started to rifle through the bag she had brought along.

"It's in desperate need of stuffed animals."

Thump, she placed a huge plush dog in the center of the room.

"See, adorable."

"What are you doing?! Commander, the living room is just going to feel even smaller—" But while Iska was protesting, the other two women started doing their own redecorating.

"I'd personally go for some flowers. And this place just won't be complete without a large-screen TV," Nene said while arranging vases and flower arrangements on the shelves. She also placed a TV that had evidently come from her own room onto the wall.

"Then I suppose I'll set up an automatic massager and a treadmill." Risya had produced a full treadmill, along with an automated massage machine.

"Mismis, what do you think of changing this wallpaper?"

"I think a floral one would be nice."

"Say, Commander, could I put a humidifier here?"

"Sure."

"What about what I want?! You three—listen to me!"

Though Iska shouted, it was all in vain as his room was transformed into an oasis of cuteness and femininity, complete with stuffed animals and the smell of sweet perfume. "Oh, my room..."

Unsurprisingly, moving around the living room was quite difficult with three women's worth of stuff in the way.

"Huh? I don't think I have anywhere to sit."

"Commander, over here, over here. Iska's bed is free," Nene said.

"Isk, another cup of tea, if you please."

"...I can't even get to the kitchen from here."

Iska was sitting on the floor and the other three—Commander Mismis, Nene, and Risya—were all cozied up to one another on top of his bed.

"Hm. It's three o'clock, right? It's too early to prep for dinner, so how about the four of us play a game? I brought one over." Risya pointed at her suitcase from where she was on the bed. "Isk, would you open up my suitcase? There should be a card game on the very top."

"Are you sure about this? I don't feel very good about looking through a woman's luggage."

"If you see something, then I suppose you'll need to do the responsible thing."

"Which is what, exactly...? Oh, is this it? You mean this Sheep and Wolf game?"

"That's it."

Once Risya took the pack of cards from him, and she started to hand out cards to the four of them.

"Make sure no one else sees your cards. It's kind of a deduction game. We're all adorable sheep, but one of us has a wolf card."

Flinch! After all of them had their cards, they all looked at each other.

"The sheep need to work together to not get eaten by the wolf. Each turn, you can use cards like 'hunter' or 'divination' to figure out who the wolf is." Risya pulled out a rulebook and opened it on the bed. "The wolf uses their villager or parent sheep card to trick the others. After three turns, we choose the most suspicious person and shoot the wolf."

"We *shoot* them?!" Commander Mismis's voice quivered. "Really, Risya?!"

"It's just a game. And, if you catch the wolf, then the sheep win. If you get it wrong, then the wolf wins. Simple, right?"

"Commander Mismis," came a whisper. Nene, who had been silent until that moment, had a glint in her eye. "You seem suspicious."

"What?"

"Yeah, it was really fishy that you shrieked just now. Almost like a real wolf."

"Wh-what are you saying, Nene?" As her cherubic face paled, Commander Mismis leaped up. "I'm not the wolf! There's no way everyone's cute, kind commander would eat sheep. Right?!"

"..."

"Nene?"

"I was watching everyone's faces carefully when we got our cards."

All four of them gripped their cards. Nene had watched their reactions from the moment they'd gotten them.

"I saw it! Commander Mismis made a face when she got her cards!"

"I—I did not! Nene, you have to believe me, I'm—"

"Okay, okay, you two calm down now." Risya's lips had curled into a grin as the two quickly became restless. "Nene has a point, and it's not as though we've determined Mismis is the wolf yet. We'll find that out through playing the game. Oh, right. I've thought of a wonderful idea."

"Ms. Risya, you have a nasty look on your face."

"What are you trying to imply, Isk? My heart is as clear as crystal," Risya responded with a wink as she stared at Mismis.

"Whoever loses should be in charge of making dinner. If the

three sheep guess the wolf's identity right, then they win. If they don't, then the wolf wins. What do you think, Mismis?"

"Why are you smiling while staring at me, Risya...?"

"Oh, no reason. We have no idea who the wolf is, after all. Right, wolf...oops, didn't mean to say that— Right, Mismis?"

"Was that on purpose?! You definitely said that to me on purpose!" Commander Mismis turned pale. Her hands shook as she held the cards, her distress as plain as day.

"Now let's start this game!"

With that, the game of Sheep and Wolf got underway. The deduction part of the game, however, had already started long ago. That was because everyone had already assumed that Mismis was the wolf.

"It's my turn! I'm using my hunter on Commander Mismis. By playing this card, whoever I point to has to confess if they're the wolf!"

"Nene?!"

"Well, you've got to be the wolf. I'm positive. So, are you?"

"...Urgh."

When Nene thrust the hunter card at her, Commander Mismis faltered. "I—I'm not the wolf!"

".......What?"

"There's no way?!"

Nene was shocked. But that could only mean...

"I know! The commander must have the villager card, then. So even if we use the hunter card on her, she can still lie. Isn't that right, Ms. Risya?"

"Right...We'll first need to steal the villager card from Mismis's hand."

"That's so mean!"

"It's my turn," Iska said. "I use my 'divination' card on Commander Mismis."

"Even you, Iska?!"

Nene, Risya, and Iska had all decided to launch a coordinated attack on Commander Mismis, but the persistent interrogation they subjected her to failed to produce any definite results in the three turns they had.

"Y-you see now...I'm not the big bad wolf!" Commander Mismis put a hand to her chest as she panted, her breaths ragged. "I'm not the wolf! I'm everyone's kind commander. I'm a harmless sheep. You have to believe me!"

Then came time for the wolf voting round. The four would vote for and shoot whoever they thought was the wolf.

It was the moment of truth.

"Commander Mismis." (Iska.)

"Commander Mismis." (Nene.)

"Mismis." (Risya.)

"Why?!"

Despite Commander Mismis's pleas, the majority had decided to shoot her (in the game).

"Urgh. You have no faith in me..."

"C'mon, Commander, hurry up and show your cards. Your wolf card—huh?!"

The moment she flipped over Mismis's cards, Nene cried out in surprise. "N-no way?! Commander Mismis *did* have a sheep card! Did we just shoot a fellow sheep?"

"No way?! Then the real wolf...it couldn't be?!"

"...It was actually me all along."

Iska, of all people, revealed his wolf card.

"It was you, Iska?!"

"Isk?! What? Then why was Mismis so shaken earlier?"

Nene and Risya were dumbfounded. Iska being the wolf came as much more of a shock than Mismis.

"Commander Mismis, why were you so shaken up?"

"That's right. Your hands were trembling."

"...I'm terrible at games, so I get nervous right away."

"That's so misleading!"

"I'm sorry!" When Nene and Risya began to pressure her, Mismis let out a wail.

"Looks like I win."

"Ugh...oh well."

"Let's go prep dinner."

The three girls headed to the dining area. Though they'd lost the game, the three of them looked winning in their aprons. Commander Mismis wore a kid's apron with cat appliqués. Nene had one on that was frilly, very fashionable and cute. Risya wore a black, genuine cook's apron that looked like it had come straight from a high-class gastronomy restaurant.

"You're so lucky, Isk. I can't believe someone in the Imperial forces' management like me is cooking for you."

"Ms. Risya, can you cook?"

"Just you watch. I'll show you the newest Imperial gourmet food trends."

The three women headed into the kitchen. As Iska watched them from the living room, the three carried on a lively conversation.

"So, can you really cook, Risya? I remember you were always eating a lunch box from the supermarket in my room."

"Heh-heh. When you're a genius like me, you can become a pro at anything with a little practice. I am *especially* good at taste-testing."

"…Taste-testing?"

"I'm also excellent at setting out plates and looking up recipes."

"None of those skills are useful!"

"Oh, that's not true. I'll set out the plates, you'll cook, Mismis. It'd be a wonderful team effo… Oh…"

Crash.

The sound of a breaking plate reached Iska's ears. He was waiting in the living room.

"Wait, Risya?!"

"Oh no. I broke Isk's large plate. This only happened because you distracted me with your chatter, Mismis."

"You're blaming it on me?!"

"I guess it's fine. Isk will never notice one missing plate."

But I will, Iska thought. Since he was a bachelor living alone, he only had a few large plates. It'd be very noticeable if he lost one of those.

"Oh……"

Crash, crash. The tragedy played out yet again. He heard another plate breaking in the dining area.

"Oh, Mismis…"

"N-no, wait?! I normally don't handle plates this big… Do you think Iska will notice all his large plates in his kitchen are gone?"

I will.

Why were they so convinced that the shattering wouldn't reach him in the living room? Even while Iska was thinking that, the three were continuing to whisper.

"…He won't notice, right?"

"It'll be fine. Iska is less observant than you'd think sometimes."

"It'll be okay, like I said. I'll just leave two autograph boards in place of the two broken plates. He'll love it."

"No, he won't!"

Things were going in a dangerous direction, Iska realized, so he quickly stood up from his seat on the floor.

"You three! I overheard the things you were saying, along with some suspicious noises."

"I-Iska?!"

"You noticed?! No, Iska, you can't come in here yet!"

"Isk, leave this to us—"

He headed right into the dining area where they were.

Then Iska saw it. Needless to say, there were some shattered plates on the ground, but most importantly, he saw what all of them were holding.

"…What's that stuff?"

A bag of consommé soup powder. (Risya.)

A pouch of instant curry sauce. (Nene)

A can of peaches. (Commander Mismis.)

All three lovely young women were holding packages of pre-made food.

"…Iska."

Suddenly, Nene teared up.

"It looks like you've made a terrible discovery about us, Iska…" Nene said.

"Nene?"

"I was going to heat this instant curry pouch up in hot water, then put it on a plate and tell you that I'd made it by hand…"

Nene looked upset. Next to her, Risya and Mismis were equally distraught.

"I was planning on telling you I spent three hours making a deluxe consommé, too…"

"I was going to say these peaches came fresh from a farm instead of from a can…"

"You can only take a lie so far!" Iska yelled and pointed at the three women's hands. "Why are you all doing this?! Ms. Risya aside, I know you two can cook!"

All Imperial force members could prepare food for themselves. Even during harsh training drills, they needed warm, fortifying meals.

"Can't the three of you...cook...?"

"What? Well..."

All of them wriggled bashfully. Nene spoke up on behalf of the other two women. "When we came by to stay here, we didn't bring cooking knives or anything. I brought regular eating utensils, but..."

"So you assumed you wouldn't be cooking?!"

Incidentally, Iska only owned a single cooking knife. Even though the three of them had gone into the kitchen at the same time, only one would have been able to get anything done.

"So we were thinking it'd be best to stick with meals that wouldn't require a knife."

"...You know...I don't think every woman needs to know how to cook, but this seems pretty bad."

They had an impromptu meeting about dinner at that point. All four concluded that barbecue would be their best bet, as they'd only have to grill the meat.

Iska went to work picking up the shards of the broken plates. Mismis lugged a military-use gas stove from the women's barracks. And Nene and Risya headed out to buy food.

"The wait's over!" Nene carried a barbecue set in a plastic bag from the supermarket.

Commander Mismis's eyes glittered the moment she laid eyes on it.

"What's this, Nene?!" she asked.

Mismis, who was generally acknowledged to be the house barbecue connoisseur, looked at the meat with wide eyes. Nene had bought high-grade cuts you didn't see every day.

"They glisten so beautifully! This is definitely the elusive, high-grade A5 meat. Supermarkets in the Imperial capital have trouble getting it, and when they can find some, it's usually too expensive to afford...Nene, how did you get this?!"

"Hm? Oh, it's my treat," Risya nonchalantly said. She was pulling cans of alcohol out of her plastic bag. "It's a barbecue party, so I figured we might as well go all out."

"But wasn't it expensive?"

"It'll be fine. I'll just claim it as an expense with headquarters." The Imperial forces higher-up had casually made a bombshell statement. "See, Mismis, even the sauce is high-grade. What do you think?"

"This is wonderful, Risya!"

"Hee-hee. I suppose it is. Once you're at my level, getting expenditures approved is easy."

Commander Mismis hugged Risya, and she didn't seem all too displeased by the attention.

"...I'll face disciplinary measures if I get caught, though."

"What?! Whatever you whispered just now sounded super ominous, Ms. Risya!"

"Ah-ha-ha! You're such a worrywart, Isk. It'll be A-OK. Worst case, I'd just tell headquarters that His Excellency ordered us to have a barbecue, and they'd immediately clam up."

"I worry for the people in headquarters who have to keep quiet for you!"

"All right, everyone!" Risya raised a beer can. "Since this is the start of our super-luxurious barbecue party, we've got to do a toast!"

Mismis and Risya each held a can of beer. Iska and Nene were underage, so they had nonalcoholic drinks…though that lasted for all but a minute before the three women stared intently at the grill.

"Here, Iska, I grilled this for you," Mismis said.

She used specialized barbecuing tongs to deftly prepare the meat. She was obviously no amateur at this and could have easily put a professional to shame.

"Commander, did I have tongs like this in my kitchen?"

"No, these are mine."

She had several sparkling ones lined up on the tabletop.

"You really have to bring your own pillow, toothbrush, and tongs with you wherever you go."

"…Is it really comparable to a pillow and toothbrush?"

"Not at all. Tongs are more important."

"How?! And who brings tongs but not a kitchen knife?!"

Mismis never stopped working as they conversed. In fact, she did an excellent job as grillmaster, keeping in mind everyone's preferences for how they liked their meat done. She even kept up with them as they ate. She handled everything perfectly and gracefully.

"…Commander, I think you could work at a barbecue restaurant."

"Oh, I actually have, part-time."

"You did for real?!"

"I once waited outside the shop of a barbecuer who was famous for not taking apprentices three days and three nights in the snow begging for him to take me on."

"Sounds like you were more serious about that than your military training…"

"On the last night, I collapsed from hunger and hypothermia, so he finally accepted me as an apprentice. I still remember all the secret techniques he taught me from that time."

"You actually *were* an apprentice?! I really want to know about the secret techniques, but that somehow feels like I'd be making a concession!"

Iska had never heard about any of this before. This had likely all happened in her military academy days before she'd officially joined as a commander.

"Nene, did you know about this?"

"Of course." The redhead sipped at her drink. "Commander Mismis went to the zoo and hit an elephant with a biscuit...and then the elephant went to war with the cats."

"Huh?"

"Uhh? Iska, why're you spinning so much...?"

From Iska's point of view, it was Nene who was swaying. She was red in the face and giggling, and she wasn't very coherent either.

"Say, Iska, this drink tastes kind of funny..."

"Wait, that's not beer, is it?!"

Instead of juice, Nene was holding the beer can that was next to Risya.

"Ha-ha...I feel kind of warm. Am I gonna turn into a star?"

"I have no idea what you're even talking about. Nene, keep it together."

"Bwop!"

"Nene?!"

She had fallen right over, her eyes unfocused. Though she wasn't her usual self, she had on the most blissful smile as she lay there.

"Ms. Risya, did you accidentally pick up Nene's drink?"

"Hm? Hold on, Isk, I'm a little busy pouring Mismis a beer."

"Wait, that's not what's important here—Ms. Risya?!"

Iska's eyes went wide when he saw the scene in front of him. Risya wasn't holding a can of beer, but instead the high-grade barbecue sauce. And she was pouring it into an empty glass.

"Wait, Ms. Risya…"

"Ah-ha-ha-ha-ha!"

"You're drunk too?!"

She continued to laugh and pour the sauce. It was then that Iska had a shocking revelation. Risya, considered the most intelligent person in the Imperial forces, became a total mess when she was drunk.

"There, Mismis, here's your beer."

It was clearly barbecue sauce. The dark brown liquid was a far cry from the amber color of beer, but alas, Iska was the only person who noticed.

"Hm?" Commander Mismis inspected the glass. She looked somewhat drowsy.

"Wait, Commander Mismis…"

"*Gulp.*"

"You actually drank it?! When did you even get drunk, Commander Mismis?! No, you can't! You'll get sick if you drink that!"

"This beer tastes kind of funny, doesn't it?"

"Because it's not beer! It's super-concentrated barbecue sauce!"

But he was too late—when it came to everything. It seemed Mismis and Risya both had low alcohol tolerance.

"Oh, looks like your glass is empty too, Risya. I'll pour you more."

"Like I said, Commander, that's the sauc—"

Flop. Right as Iska was saying that, something made of fabric fell onto his head.

"Uh…a jacket?"

"Hmm…The barbecuing is making me feel kind of warm." Risya had taken off her jacket and was now in just her shirt. And— right before Iska's very eyes—she was slowly starting to unbutton that as well…

"Let's strip!"

"No! Ms. Risya, you need to come back to your senses! What happened to your usual intelligent self?!"

"Ah-ha-ha-ha. What are you saying, chocolate waffle? I'm always very intelligent."

"Is my name Chocolate Waffle now?!"

Risya had already undone her fourth button. Though she was slim, her breasts were exposed in all their glamour, so Iska had no choice but to look away.

"Ms. Risya, your jacket...!"

"Oh, Iska, how could you ogle at Ms. Risya like that?"

He heard Nene's voice come from behind him. Before he could even turn around, Nene had latched onto his back while still on the ground.

"Nene?!"

"Hee-hee. You're so cute, Iska."

Nene wore a giant smile as she kept a tight hold on him. It seemed she hadn't sobered up yet, since she was still red in the face.

"I guess this is better than Ms. Risya trying to strip..."

"Heeey, how about we do a staring contest? If you laugh, you lose! Ah-ha-ha-ha-ha-hah!"

"We haven't even started and you're already laughing!"

Risya stripped when drunk. Nene apparently was a happy drunk. And then...

"My stuffed animal!"

"I'm not your stuffed animal!"

This time Mismis latched onto Iska's arm.

"Uh-whaaa? Was my body pillow always this hard?"

"Please don't mistake me for one."

"Zzz..."

"Wait, are you really falling asleep?! Don't use my arm as a pillow! Agh! Everyone, please come back to your senses!"

But Iska's pleading was in vain.

"Time to start the pillow fight!"

Risya, her shirt still wide open, had grabbed Mismis's stuffed animal and gotten to her feet.

"Oh, Riiisya, that's mine—"

With a loud *thwump*, Mismis was struck in the face. Risya had been the one to throw the stuffed animal, of course.

"…"

"C-Commander? Are you okay?"

"Now you've done it!"

Commander Mismis grinned as she stood up. She threw the stuffed animal right back at Risya.

"Take that!"

However, she was so unsteady that she hadn't been able to aim well. The stuffed animal sailed through the air—in a completely different direction from Risya—and hit the wall of the living room.

She'd lobbed it right at the emergency alarm. Each Imperial forces room had an emergency switch, and Mismis had the one in Iska's.

"Oh……"

"I won!"

The instant after Mismis shouted in glee, the alarm went off.

"Emergency! An emergency has occurred!"

The siren wailed. Iska's room was bathed in red light, making it as obvious as could be that his room was the origin of the supposed problem.

"Oh noooo!"

"What's the emergency?"

"This only happened because of the stuffed animal you threw, Commander!"

"...Zzz."

"You fell back asleep?! Urgh...we—we need to stop the alarm!"

This was the forces' barracks, so armed soldiers were sure to come running over in mere minutes.

"Stop the notification system—"

"Ah-ha-ha, this is so fun, Iska," Nene said.

"Nene?! W-wait! Please! We need to fix this situation first!"

Nene, the happy drunk that she was, had chosen then to latch onto Iska's arm as well, and she wasn't letting go.

"Nuh-uh! You're mine!"

"Oh my. That looks like fun, Isk. I'd like to join in, too."

Now even Risya was holding on to him from behind. He was only a few centimeters shy of the switch, if he stretched his arms. He was just a finger's length away...

"Let go of me, you two!"

"Ah-ha-ha-ha-ha!"

"Your back is so warm, Isk!"

Then someone kicked down his door. The armed emergency response squad had just arrived.

"Did the alarm come from here?!"

"We're here now, so you're safe. There's nothing to—"

The soldiers were also carrying guns. And what they witnessed in Iska's room were the three merry women acting very unladylike.

"..."

There was Risya, who had taken off her jacket and unbuttoned most of her shirt, then Nene, who was laughing and rolling around on the floor. Even Commander Mismis had removed her jacket at some point, too.

"..."

This was awkward.

Iska suspected the armed soldiers had made some unfortunate assumption about the scene before them.

"I-it's not what it looks like. We just..." Iska waved his hands around desperately, but the soldiers had no mercy.

"Inform HQ that we've secured three women and have apprehended a suspect."

"A suspect? Do you mean me?!"

"You'll be coming with us on charges of sexual misconduct."

"I haven't done anything!"

Incident report.

Imperial soldier Iska

Investigated by Imperial headquarters on suspicion of sexual misconduct and abducting three women in his room.

Note: Suspect has denied all charges.

―――――――――

Meanwhile, in another land...in the Paradise of Witches, the Nebulis Sovereignty's palace...

"..."

"Uh, um, Lady Alice...?"

Rin felt in her bones that her beloved lady, Alice, was in a terrible mood. The attendant peered at Alice's face to check on her.

"...What is the meaning of this?"

Aliceliese Lou Nebulis was a beautiful girl with bright golden hair...but at that moment, she looked grim.

"Rin, this incident report is from yesterday, isn't it?"

"Y-yes."

"Do you believe the Imperial soldier Iska in this report is the same Iska?"

"...It's very likely."

"I see."

Alice was silently fuming.

She wasn't taking out her frustrations on Rin, of course, but her attendant could feel some of it sneaking into the edges of her voice.

"Rin, what do you make of this?"

"Uh, uhh..."

She didn't know how to respond.

The Imperial swordsman Iska was their enemy—not to mention Alice's greatest foe. As far as Rin was concerned, she hoped the investigation would last forever.

"Are you telling me that Iska is a pervert? That's unbelievable. He would *never*!"

Alice, on the other hand, saw things differently. She seemed outraged at the Empire for their silly charges against her dear rival.

"What do you think, Rin?"

"R-right...um..."

She hoped that he'd remain in custody—but if she said this, she knew Alice would turn on her.

"I would like to state that the Imperial swordsman is an enemy of our country...but I doubt he would do anything that would go against human morals."

"Yes, exactly!" Alice balled her hands into fists. "I smell a plot!"

"A plot?"

"Iska would never do anything so perverse. Something must have disrupted the Empire's internal state of affairs. Someone must be trying to frame him. That has to be it!"

"Uh-huh..."

"Rin, prepare the bail money to free Iska posthaste!"

"What?! You're going to help the enemy?!"

"Yes, and I'm doing this *because* he's the enemy."

Alice's resolve was firm.

"I can't stand by as the person I need to settle things with on the battlefield is held on charges of sexual misconduct. I mean—"

She turned to the window, staring to the south, straight at where the Imperial territory would be.

"Iska would never spurn me and lay a hand on another woman!"

"Someone's going to get things all wrong if you put it like that!"

"But he's my rival."

Alice was the very image of seriousness. Then again, Rin was right about Alice's choice of words.

"Iska and I are tied by the fate of the stars (for a rematch)!"

"And now you make it sound like you're an actual couple!"

"Anyway! What in the world are you doing when you have me around, Iska?!"

Several days later, Alice nodded in satisfaction when she received news that he'd been acquitted and released.

File 04

*Our Last Crusade or
Alice's Betrothal War
(Her Happily Ever After)?*

Secret File

CONFIDENTIAL

"This is terrible, Iska! It's a disaster!"

"Right, sure, it is. Anyway, about today's joint drill—"

"Uh, wait, Iska? Please listen to me!"

"Commander Mismis, whenever you say something's a disaster, it never actually is."

The Imperial capital Yunmelngen.

In the sector three military base within the city, Iska took his time turning around.

"If you found an abandoned cat outside, then take it to the consultation office. It should be fine."

"It's not that!"

"Then if you've found a drunk lying down outside the base, call the military police…"

"It's not anything like that either!"

The petite commander shook her head.

She was Commander Mismis Klass. Despite her baby face and tendency to act like a small animal, she was actually a full-grown adult. She was also a member of the Imperial forces and the one who kept Unit 907 together as its commander.

"This really is huge news. It'll have the Imperial Forces in an uproar for sure!"

"...If it were really that important, then wouldn't it come directly from headquarters?"

"I got my hands on an exclusive scoop! See here!"

She held a periodical that had been handed around the capital.

The Astonishing Truth Revealed!
The Nebulis Sovereignty Princess Has a Lover!

"Uh..."

"Right, isn't this something?"

"Oh, I see. You mean the article below that. 'Kittens Born at Capital's Sector Three Café'..."

"No, not that! The one about the Nebulis princess in love!"

The Nebulis Sovereignty was, to summarize it succinctly, the enemy that the Imperial forces were at war with. The Empire that Iska and his companions were part of were in an ongoing century-long war with the Paradise of Witches, the Nebulis Sovereignty.

"...Is it really such a big deal that an enemy princess has a lover?"

"A huge deal! Look at the rumors! Plus, the boyfriend must be just as big of a deal. Maybe he's royalty from another country somewhere!" Commander Mismis grew more and more animated. "If they actually get together officially, then the Sovereignty might end up with a powerful ally. They might become an even bigger threat to us."

"Oh, you've got a point."

Iska wanted to ignore that and chalk the news up to being part of the rumor mill, but she was right—there was a possibility this would affect the Imperial forces.

Now he could understand why Mismis was so panicked.

"So one question. Why'd you come straight to me with this news? Wouldn't you normally head over to the headquarters to tell them first?"

"Well, because your photo's in it…In the article."

"Come again?"

There was a picture of him? In an article about a Nebulis Sovereignty princess having a boyfriend?

"What do you mean?"

"See, here. Your photo is on the side of the article. The back profile of the person they're claiming is her boyfriend looks just like yours."

"Oh, is this another joke…huh?……"

Their back profile did indeed resemble his. That looked like his messy black hair and slim-yet-muscular back.

…It really does look like me.

…Those even look like my clothes.

Iska had a jacket that looked awfully similar to the one in the photo. He recognized the streets in the background. It was the business district of the neutral city Ain, which Iska often visited.

"Iska, you haven't betrayed the Empire and been out consorting with the Nebulis Sovereignty, have you…?"

"S-stop right there, Commander! It does look like me, that's for sure, but still!" Iska waved his hands around in a panic as Mismis eyed him suspiciously. "It's someone else. Someone who resembles me a lot."

"…Really?"

"I sure don't remember doing that. And how could I be the lover of an enemy princess? What kind of Imperial force member would do that?"

Despite what he'd said, Iska did have an inkling about the news. He actually was acquainted with a Sovereignty princess. But he sure wasn't her lover—they were rivals on the battlefield.

"But what if Alice...? No, she wouldn't do this. It must be a mistake."

It was preposterous to think that Alice would ever report to someone else that Iska was her boyfriend. In other words, it had to be a doppelganger. That was what Iska concluded, at least.

"Plus, I'm pretty average-looking, anyway. I could appear to be anyone else from behind."

"Hmm...I suppose. Yeah, you're right. There's no way you'd be the boyfriend of an enemy princess."

Commander Mismis accepted that.

"I'm sorry, Iska. The person in the picture looks so similar to you that I had to ask."

"No, it's all right. Sometimes coincidences happen. He just happened to resemble me."

Iska nodded slowly as he looked at the photo in the article.

There was no way—he couldn't imagine it was actually him, even in his wildest dreams.

———

Several days earlier.

The Paradise of Witches, the Nebulis Sovereignty.

A room within the palace.

"...This is bad. This is extremely bad. Her Majesty will be here soon!"

Alice was frightened at the prospect of a visit from her mother, the queen.

"Rin, the door is closed, isn't it?"

"Y-yes, Lady Alice."

"Excellent job. Please shut the windows just to be sure as well."

Aliceliese Lou Nebulis was a beautiful princess with brilliant golden locks. The Imperial forces feared her as the Ice Calamity Witch, and the Imperial swordsman Iska shared a mutual rivalry with her, though they kept this secret from everyone else.

And as for Alice…

Once a month, she was subject to a day of fear.

"Lady Alice."

Rin, Alice's attendant, pointed at the door and turned back to her.

"It is time. It seems Her Majesty has arrived."

"No, Rin! You absolutely cannot open it!"

She fled deeper into her living room and hid behind a large bookcase. Only her head was peeking out from her hiding place.

"I'm out right now. That's what you should tell her!"

"Even if I did, you were just at a conference meeting."

"Th-then…I'm sick. Cough, cough…see, my head feels so heavy, and I think I feel a fever coming on. Oh, I might fall right over on the spot!"

"But you're the picture of health."

"R-regardless, I can't do this. I don't intend to see Mother toda—"

"I can hear you, Alice."

"Eep!"

The door was forced open. Oh no. She'd made a miscalculation— the queen had a duplicate key to the room. When Alice realized her fatal error, she let out a deep sigh.

"Mother..."

"Good morning, Alice. You look uneasy today. Is something the matter?"

Nebulis VIII. The queen—the greatest witch among the witches—was feared by the Imperial forces, but she was beautiful, elegant, and beloved by the Sovereignty's people. And she was Princess Alice's mother.

"Whew. Carrying these around is so tiring."

Thump. The queen had placed a mountain of photo albums on Alice's desk.

"You don't mean to tell me..."

"Here is this month's list of prospective candidates to meet with."

"Nooo!" she wailed and backed away.

Yes. This was the day Alice feared each month—when she was given a list of her prospective suitors.

"Mother! I haven't even had a boyfriend yet! It's much too soon to meet with marriage in mind!"

"Alice, I'm going through the trouble to ensure we find a good romantic prospect for you." The queen picked up one album. "As a seventeen-year-old princess, you really should find a boyfriend. The palace is in agreement about this matter. In fact, it is a royal decree."

"...Urgh!" Alice was still very serious about her feelings on the matter, though a royal decree had a very persuasive effect on her. "While I may be a princess, Mother, I'm also a regular girl. You make it sound as though I will simply agree to these marriage meetings, but I don't intend to—"

"This month, you will see three candidates."

"I don't get any say in this?!"

"Alice, this will bring you happiness. Also, there is a crowd simply itching to meet you."

She received marriage proposals from other nations on a near daily basis from royalty, entrepreneurs, and the wealthy. Though Alice's status as possible heir to the throne was attractive, her seventeen-year-old charm was even more alluring.

"But why just me? You don't make Elletear and Sisbell do this."

Alice was the second born of three sisters. Though she had both a younger and an older sister close to her in age, she'd never heard of either of them being ordered to go to prospective marriage meetings.

"Why is it just me, Mother?"

"Elletear is overseas visiting other nations, so she couldn't possibly attend marriage meetings when she is away from the castle."

"But Sisbell is here."

"It's impossible." The queen shook her head plainly. "She already doesn't leave her room as it is."

"……Right."

Indeed. The third princess, Sisbell, was an extremely shy shut-in. Alice hadn't seen Sisbell leave her room for nearly a month. If anyone tried to force her into marriage talks, she would have refused to leave her room for an entire year.

"So I'm afraid you'll have to make up for your sisters and do three people's worth of courting, Alice. I'm counting on you."

"Three meetings, though? I have to do three people's work?! That isn't fair, Mother!"

"I have a conference to attend now," the queen said, not even hearing Alice's protests as she exited the room.

Alice and Rin were left to their own devices.

"Wh-why is this happening…?"

"Lady Alice, I understand how you feel, but there are some things you just must accept." Rin looked very serious as she picked up the album. "You are Her Majesty's beloved daughter. She is simply hoping that you will find a wonderful partner."

"I know that, but still…"

She staggered onto the sofa in front of her.

"I don't think love should be so contrived. I don't want to meet this way—I want to have a fateful encounter!"

Alice was at a sensitive age, so of course she would have ideas about what love should be like. If she was going to fall in love, she wanted it to be dramatic, something straight from a dream.

"Hmph…"

"Please don't pout. They're your prospective partners, so you must choose them yourself."

Even as Alice sulked, Rin was in the midst of picking out suitable matches.

"What do you think of this guy? He's a doctor from a neighboring nation. He's young and graduated top of his class from medical school. I would feel much more at ease having a doctor around if something were to happen to you."

"I don't care who I meet with…I'll turn them down anyway, so you can pick, Rin."

Alice sprawled out on the sofa. She absentmindedly stared at the pile of albums on the table.

"Say, Rin, doesn't it seem like there are a lot more offers this month?"

"Oh, that would be because—" Rin stopped as she was turning a page in an album and clapped her hands together as though she'd recalled something. "I believe that is because a photo of you was revealed to the public when applications opened last month."

"A photo?"

"Yes. It was one from when you went on the trip to the beach. See, this one."

"But that would make it a swimsuit shot!"

Alice leaped up. She opened the album with the same gusto and stared at one of the pictures.

"Is this...?!"

The photo featured a white coast and a blue ocean that sparkled like a jewel, as well as Alice in a swimsuit, elegantly looking up at the brilliant sunlight as it blazed down upon her...

"Wh-wh-what is this?!"

"As I said, that came from the month before last, when the beaches were opened."

"That's not what I mean! I don't recall anyone taking this picture of me!"

One of her subordinates had likely sneakily taken it. But Alice wasn't red in the face simply because of the swimsuit.

"This was a private trip, wasn't it?"

"Yes."

"And they said I could relax, so I remembered thinking I could wear a slightly trendy swimsuit..."

As a result of wearing a somewhat skimpier swimsuit...Alice's ample bosom seemed close to falling out. Her hips were also exposed for all to see, and her wet golden locks clung seductively to her pale skin.

...I wasn't aware of this at all.

...Was I really so scantily dressed?

Even from her perspective, it seemed very risqué. Alice turned red from the unexpected embarrassment.

"Wait, this picture was made public to the marriage proposal applicants?!"

"Yes. The cabinet ministers unanimously approved it."

"What kind of meetings are they holding in secret?!"

"The moment this swimsuit photo was publicized, you received an explosive number of matchmaking requests from all over the world. In that respect, it was very effective."

"That doesn't make me happy in the slightest!"

She slammed her hand on the table. Alice's swimsuit photo—her bare skin exposed to daylight—had attracted a pack of libidinous men.

"...I'm so over this."

"Lady Alice, your picture made a huge splash."

"This is so idiotic! Everyone involved is a disgrace! I want nothing to do with this!" Alice howled and once again hurled herself onto the sofa.

On the day of the marriage talks, Alice waited for the prospective partner she was to meet in the palace lounge.

"Lady Alice, he should be here soon."

"...Ahh. I do *not* want to do this."

Though Alice was dressed up specially for her betrothal meetings, sitting in a chair was enough to elicit a sigh from her.

"Rin, it's three people today?"

"Yes. If you find one who seems perfect among them, I'm sure no one would object to ending things early."

"...Right."

She glanced up at the ceiling. It would be only slightly longer until the appointed person was to come.

"Okay, I've decided, Rin!"

"Lady Alice?" Rin looked up at her lady, who had stood up. "What's suddenly gotten into you?"

"I've found my motivation. If it is an order from Mother, then

I must obey it, so I cannot remain despondent forever. Also, you must feel ashamed of my behavior, as my attendant."

"Lady Alice!" Rin's voice trembled from emotion. "So you've finally come around! And I'm so happy you are concerned about me!"

"Of course I am. So, all I must do is decide whether they live up to my expectations as a boyfriend?"

"Yes! Please take as much time as you need to consider them!"

"...Right, of course."

She laughed under her breath. However, Rin was so greatly moved that she failed to notice this.

Knock. They heard a sound from the other side of the door. It seemed the first suitor had arrived.

"Well then, Lady Alice, I shall make myself scarce in the back room. I will watch over the meeting through the camera!"

"Just leave things to me."

Alice waited for Rin to leave, then called out to the person beyond the door, "Please come in."

"I'm pleased to make your acquaintance, Princess Aliceliese. It is an honor to meet with you."

A slim young man wearing a formal white suit had entered. He had a magnificent career working as both an entrepreneur and magazine model. His striking, deeply chiseled features gave him a clean and dignified look.

"It is nice to meet you. You may call me Alice."

"Well then...allow me to say once again that it is a pleasure to meet you, Princess Alice. You looked beautiful in your photo of course, but it hardly did you justice now that I am seeing your beauty in person."

"Oh, what an honor." She smiled as she placed her hand over her mouth.

The photo he must have been talking about had to be the one of her in a swimsuit. But her logical side won out and she kept herself from commenting on it.

"Well, to get right to the point, I have my own method of evaluating you."

"Evaluating me?"

"Yes. Please look above."

"Above?"

The young businessman did as he was told. A block of ice shaped just like a hammer dropped down on him that instant.

Thwack.

It made a painful sound as it scored a direct hit.

"...Uh, ngh."

After being struck in the head by the ice hammer, the suitor fell over. He'd fainted.

"So, you failed. Next!"

"What are you doing, Lady Alice?!" Rin leaped out from the back room. "Why are you attacking your suitor with your astral power?!"

"I'm not attacking him. I'm evaluating him."

"Evaluating him?"

"Yes. Just take a look at him."

"...I see that he has a huge lump on his head and that he's unconscious."

"Yes. And that won't do!" Alice firmly declared as she pointed at the collapsed young man. "Any romantic interest of mine needs to meet my minimum standard of strength."

Alice wasn't simply a princess. She was the princess of the Nebulis Sovereignty, the land of the most powerful astral mages. Any partner of hers would need to be able to keep up with her in might.

"Plenty of men may look put-together on the outside, but they must be equally as capable within. I have a duty to do all in my power to choose an appropriate suitor!"

"But why would you put all your efforts into attacking them?!... Well, I know you were quite kind and held back on him, but..."

Alice had once singlehandedly destroyed an entire Imperial force base. If she were to go all out against anyone, it would likely have to be a Saint Disciple, the highest-ranked combatants in the Empire. Alice had held back considerably when she'd made the lump of ice just earlier.

"I considered using an ice blade...but it looks like the hammer was the right choice."

"Are you planning to drench the lounge in blood?!"

Rin picked the man up and held him steady on her shoulder as she let out a disappointed sigh.

"Regardless, no more of that! Even if you are evaluating them, you cannot knock them unconscious by attacking them by surprise—it's unreasonable!"

"Oh, I can't?"

"That's right...Anyway, I'll need to take Lord Cyrus to the medical room."

"Cyrus?"

"That is his name! As in the man I'm currently carrying!"

Incidentally, in the event the young man successfully evaded her attack, Alice had planned to commend him and ask him his name. Unfortunately, he'd fallen with a single blow, so she'd never had the opportunity.

"You're right. I shouldn't have let things end without so much as asking their name."

"So you've realized that, then?"

"I'll ask the next one's suitors name before attacking him."

"But that's just a duel!"

"It's a betrothal interview."

"You absolutely cannot do that!...Oh, Lady Alice, please treat the second one like an actual meeting. Please don't attack him immediately!"

"..."

"Aren't you going to say anything?"

"Fiiine!" Alice nodded in resignation. "If I must. If my dear attendant goes as far as to ask me for that, then I suppose I must acquiesce as your lady."

"Please do."

As Rin carried the (first) suitor, she headed into the back room once again.

After some time, there came a second knock at the door.

"Please come in."

"Well, I'm pleased to make your acquaintance, Princess Aliceliese. It is an honor to meet with you!"

It was the second suitor.

A large man of staggering size had walked through the door. He had once been a well-known athlete and used his fame to pivot into politics. The young man was seen as an up-and-comer even in the political sphere.

"It is nice to meet you. You may call me Alice."

"Well, Princess Alice, you looked beautiful in your photo of course, but it hardly did you justice now that I am seeing your beauty in person."

"Oh, what an honor." She smiled as she placed her hand over her mouth. She had a sneaking suspicion that he'd spouted nearly exactly the same line as the first suitor.

"Please do sit down, um...Mr. Bruno."

"Well, if you'll excuse me."

The young politician who sat across from her was so muscular that his suit seemed about to burst at the seams, and the chair he sat in almost seemed cramped.

"I heard that you are a politician, but it seems that you're quite well-built."

"Ha-ha-ha! Though I've retired, I still keep up my former training regimen!"

He had once been a combat sport fighter, so his upper arms were twice as large as Alice's. Even his chest was surprisingly bulky.

"They called me 'the steel strongman' when I was active."

Alice didn't say a word.

"Oh, is something the matter, Princess Alice?"

"No. I was just so impressed, I'm embarrassed to say I couldn't help but admire you." Alice placed her hand on her cheek as she answered. "So, Mr. Bruno."

"Yes?"

"Can that body of yours stop a speeding bullet?"

"……Come again?"

"Well, a handgun wouldn't be enough, so let's say that you withstood fire from one of the Imperial standard issue TH87-type automatic rifles. How many bullets do you think you could handle?"

"Um, Princess Alice…What do you possibly mean by that?"

"As you are well aware, the Sovereignty is in the middle of a war with the Imperial forces."

The war was on again off again, more or less. Though they were currently at a standstill, they would never know when the balance would fall apart.

"Why, the Imperial forces may invade the palace at some point."

"…Oh, yes."

"And if Imperial soldiers were to come here with their guns at the ready, you might even take a bullet."

"What?!" The man's expression abruptly shifted on his tan face.

This was going just as she expected. He had likely only applied as a suitor because he'd been charmed by her physique in that photo, so he wasn't prepared for this. To propose to a Nebulis Sovereignty princess meant making an enemy out of the Imperial forces.

"If you were to marry me, you might be targeted by the Empire."

"Uh, urgh?!"

He looked perplexed at that.

…I'm sorry.

…Of course that's quite an overexaggerated worry.

Secretly, Alice was both grinning and apologizing to him internally. Though she was being quite dramatic informing him about the dangers he would face, she doubted the current situation would progress into a full-blown war. She was simply testing his mentality. She just wanted to see how prepared he was for this.

"Would you protect me?"

"O-of course!" the politician howled. He thumped his chest as though he were amping himself up. "I would protect you even if it turns the Imperial forces against me!"

"You really would?"

"I would!"

"My, that's wonderful," she answered with a smile. "Then please allow me to make sure of that."

"Huh?"

"Please look up."

"Up?"

The young politician did just that.

Just then, a block of ice shaped like a hammer flew down at his forehead.

"Ice?!...Urgh! That's nothing!"

He leaped from his seat and rolled onto the floor, skillfully dodging the attack. It seemed his claims about being a famous athlete were true. His reflexes were much quicker than the average person's.

"Wow! That's amazing, Mr. Bruno!" Even Alice was surprised by this. She nodded at him as a genuine compliment to his skill. "Please excuse my rudeness. They say seeing is believing, after all. I believe that has proven you really were telling the truth, Mr. Bruno."

"Haah, haah...o-of course I was."

He stood back up. Though he was out of breath, his face was as cheery as an athlete who had just won a match. "Do you see now? I would be a perfect partner for you—"

"Well, shall we try another?"

"Huh?"

"It's not as though the enemy would limit themselves to a single attack." Alice smiled.

The moment light gathered at her fingertips, an even larger block of ice flew down from the air with great force.

Thunk. The larger block hit him right in the head when he was least expecting it.

"...Uh, ngh."

Her suitor fell to the floor upon being struck in the head with the ice.

"Oh, what a shame. The next one may come in."

"What do you think you're doing, Lady Alice?!" Rin appeared

again from the back room. "As I said earlier, you cannot attack your suitors—"

"Oh, no, Rin. I wasn't doing that this time."

"What?"

"I figured out a process. First, I inquired whether he was prepared. Then he said he was."

She had asked if he was prepared to have the Imperial forces as his enemy. And he'd replied in the affirmative.

"In which case, don't you think he needs the abilities to make good on his intentions?"

"*Haah...*"

"So I attacked him."

"Therein lies the problem! And you didn't do it once but twice..."

"I'm sure I can keep it up, too."

"I'm not worried about you, Lady Alice! I pity the suitors!" Rin collected the former athlete from the ground. "I'll take him to the medical room, too."

"It's necessary. I mean, Rin, if a man you've never met before told you he would protect you with his life, what would you think?"

"He would seem suspicious, so I would ignore him."

"And what if he begins following you around?"

"A man who is weaker than me wouldn't be able to protect me, so I'd test his abilities... wait? I see. Now that I think about it, I would want to attack him, too..."

"You get it. I really ought to confirm it for myself."

Rin reluctantly agreed. Alice crossed her arms and chuckled.

"So, on to the next one. Rin, please take Mr. Bruno to the medical room. I will prepare myself to attack the third one."

"Please at least call it a betrothal meeting..."

"I wonder how long the next one will last. If he can make it through five attacks, then we'll say he has a fighting chance."

"This isn't a battle, you know!"

Then the third suitor arrived.

The last one for the day.

"Hey, it's an honor to meet ya, Princess Alice. The moment I set my eyes on your swimsuit bod—"

"Please leave."

"Gaah?!"

The instant Alice opened her mouth, she silenced the well-built middle-aged man by hitting him with a block of ice.

"Ugh! He just liked that swimsuit photo! And he was looking at me so indecently!"

"W-well...It seems the last one got what he deserved." Rin hauled the third suitor to the medical room.

The last man happened to be from another country's royal family, but that didn't intimidate Alice.

"Ah, I'm so tired. Rin, I've fulfilled my quota, haven't I?"

"Y-yes..."

A businessman, a politician, a member of a royal line—all men were wealthy and had impressive social standings, but that wasn't anything special as far as Alice was concerned.

It was all wrong. What she actually wanted was...

"I've finally figured it out today, Rin. I've decided I will never do a betrothal meeting again!"

"B-but what will Her Majesty say...?"

"I'll convince Mother."

"Are you truly serious?!"

"I am. And I will demonstrate how serious I am to her as well!"

She gallantly turned around, throwing away the albums of potential suitors as she made her firm declaration.

*　　*　　*

She was in the Queen's Space.

"Mother, I am fed up with this betrothal system!"

She had called upon the queen, who had just finished a meeting, to loudly declare this before her.

"I've had enough of meeting strange and unfamiliar men!"

"……Alice?" The queen turned around. "Is this about the marriage talks from earlier?"

"Yes, Mother. I do not believe I should be bound by these outdated traditions. A princess must be free to do as she wills and be more progressive!"

"…Oh?"

"…is what Rin said," Alice concluded.

"I never said anything at all! Please, Lady Alice, don't say whatever you like and then put the words into my mouth!" Rin hid behind Alice in a panic. "Your Majesty, please! Uh, um…Lady Alice was speaking her own mind, and I would never make such outrageous—"

"You are exactly right."

"……Huh?"

The queen nodded deeply. Alice was so shocked that she turned behind her to share a glance with Rin.

"What do you mean, Mother?"

"It is as you say, Alice. I believe you are not wrong to say that this tradition is outdated."

Alice had been convinced that she would be scolded, but it seemed she had done quite the opposite and moved the queen.

"Alice, Rin, I do not know whether you are aware, but this betrothal system was created when we were still called witches."

There was a time period when astral mages such as them were persecuted.

"A princess subject to rumors of being a frightening witch will not have a fateful encounter with a lover. That was why the royal family started promising wealth and status to fiancé applicants from other countries. This started decades ago."

"Uh-huh…"

"But times have changed. Our country has grown into a major power, and we have received acknowledgement that astral mages deserve human rights." The queen swept her eyes across the room as she continued proudly, "Now you receive marriage proposals from other countries without having to pay large sums of money. It has become easier for you to seek out a partner for yourself in this day and age."

"Y-yes! That's right, Mother. That was what I wished to tell you!"

They were in agreement. Alice felt all the dissatisfaction she'd had earlier disappear.

"Oh, and…" The queen cleared her throat. She stared at her beloved daughter. "Though I admit I am biased as your mother, you are beautiful and wise, Alice. I am sure you will find the person you are fated for without all these betrothal negotiations."

"Oh, Mother dearest!" Filled with emotion, Alice ran to her mother. She threw out her arms and gave the queen a firm hug. "You really do understand, Mother!"

"Yes. However…" As her daughter hugged her, the queen's eyes glinted for a second. "I need to have peace of mind as your mother…"

"Come again?"

"I'd like you to introduce me to the young man you pick. I will feel much more at ease, and I promise not to speak of betrothal meetings if you do that."

"Uh, um…wha…?"

"You said it yourself—that you would find your own partner. You said that because you were sure you'd find him, correct?"

"Wh-why, of course!"

Though Alice nodded, she had broken out into an unrelenting cold sweat.

A fated match? There was no way. It wasn't as though Alice could find someone just because she'd set her mind to it.

"I'm so looking forward to it, Alice. I wonder what he will be like when you introduce us."

"Ah—ah-ha-ha...right..."

Alice returned to her chambers.

"...The situation has grown ever more dire." Alice let out a sigh. "I thought I was just going to voice my opposition, but it seems that I've promised to find myself a boyfriend immediately."

"Her Majesty completely drove you into a corner!"

Rin had warned her as much. The attendant poured Alice tea and sighed. "Her Majesty has given you quite some motivation. If you find a boyfriend, she will allow you to end the marriage talks. But to put it another way, until you find yourself one, they will continue."

"What more did I expect? She really has done a spectacular job cornering me..."

"You were being ridiculous from the start, Lady Alice."

"...Ahh. What will I do?"

She'd been too naive in her calculations, just as Rin had warned her.

She was up against the Nebulis queen herself. Alice knew her mother was clever and experienced, so she should have come up with a better plan from the start.

"Please help me, Rin. At this rate, I'll have even more marriage meetings next month, and I'll lose sleep from the stress."

"Lady Alice, you're quite shameless, so I'm sure you'll be able to sleep just fine."

"That wasn't what I wanted you to say. Please, just come here."

She motioned for Rin to come to the table in the living room. The two of them settled into their seats and began their strategy session.

—First order of business: abolition of the marriage talks.

—Method: convince the queen.

Things were clear up to this point.

In order to make a persuasive argument, Alice would need to find a boyfriend.

"But what will you do? Will you find yourself someone immediately?"

"...Right." Alice thought in silence for some time, then came to a conclusion:

"What if I fabricated one?"

"You do realize you are up against Her Majesty. She will surely ask for proof."

"I've used all avenues available to me!"

"You're giving up much too quickly!" Rin brought her hand to her temple and let out a sigh. "Then...let's think about this from the beginning. We should figure out what you're looking for in a suitor first."

"Right."

Now that Rin mentioned it, she'd never actually voiced her preferences out loud before.

"I suppose it's important that it is someone I can respect, first of all."

"Could you put that in more concrete terms?"

"I'd like someone with a backbone. I don't want him to be a yes-man, so I'd like him to have the guts to tell me when I'm wrong."

"I understand why you want that...but, Lady Alice, I think there may be only a hundred men in the world with the guts to argue with you face-to-face. "

As a Nebulis Sovereignty princess, she was also an influential world leader. How many men wouldn't be intimidated by Alice, considering that?

"And I'd like him to be strong, of course. Someone strong enough to fight with me if I were to use all my strength."

"That restricts the pool to about ten people in the entire world!"

"Those are my two criteria."

"Must your standards be so high...I'm afraid you may well never find a fiancé."

"And it will be important to share the same interests."

"Now you're adding more requirements?! And didn't you just say you only had two?!"

"Well, I can't help that I came up with another one."

Alice was quite serious about this. Since this had to do with her all-important love life, she needed to put her whole mind into it.

"And I'd like him to be thoughtful. Since he will be dating me, he must be openhearted—that's crucial."

"Your standards are too high!"

"But I find this very important for the search."

She didn't want him to be intimidated by her. And she would like someone who was strong enough to fight her when she was truly trying. And someone with the same hobbies who was sensitive...

"Yes. For example, someone like Iska."

"Iska?"

"...Oh."

She'd let that slip out. Even Alice's eyes went wide from surprise when she realized she'd said his name unconsciously.

"Oh, my? What did I just...?"

No, wait. Someone did exist—she had the perfect boy who fit all of her criteria already.

"Rin, I've found him!"

"What?...Wait, you don't mean?! I believe I heard a most reprehensible name just now...!" Rin widened her eyes. "Wait, Lady Alice, you can't say it! If what I'm thinking is—"

"I have Iska!"

"It has to be him?! You cannot!"

"...But he fits all my requirements."

The former Saint Disciple of the Empire, Iska. He'd been the only Imperial soldier to battle Alice at full strength and leave the match in a stalemate. But when they'd met at a neutral city, they'd been in agreement about what their favorite things were—almost like siblings—and he was also easygoing.

...Now that I think about it...

...He really does meet all the criteria perfectly.

He fulfilled every last qualification Alice sought in a man. But then again, the Empire and Sovereignty were in the middle of a war. Also, Alice didn't want Iska as a boyfriend anyway—she considered him a rival in battle.

"...But I may be able to use this. This may convince Mother." Alice nodded astutely, as though trying to convince herself it would work. "Say, Rin, do you happen to have Iska's picture? I believe you had one you took in the neutral city, right?"

"What are you planning to do with it?"

"I'm going to pretend I've found myself a boyfriend. I'll use it to report to Mother."

She took a deep breath.

"Yes, this is all a sham. Iska and I wouldn't ever fall in love, even if the world turned upside down."

"Yes, quite right. That's good...but why is your face so red, Lady Alice?"

"Y-you're just imagining it!"

As her attendant stared at her face, Alice quickly turned away.

"I could never fathom falling in love with Iska."

"I—I see..."

"Yes, that's right! I don't have any feelings for him whatsoever!"

"Why are you repeating yourself, then?"

"____"

"I find your sudden silence more suspicious. Please, Lady Alice!"

The Queen's Space.

Alice ran to the queen carrying a photo in her hand, panting.

"Mother, I shall introduce him to you now!"

"What is it, Alice? You've been making quite a few trips here today. And who are you introducing me to?"

"This is the man I love!"

She raised the photo high into the air. Yes, the only one she had of Iska. Since Alice also appeared at the edge of the photo, it was proof that they did know each other.

"You mean this boy with black hair in this photo?"

"That's right!"

"But you can only see his back in this."

Alice's mother still seemed somewhat dubious as she looked at it. She had promised Alice that she would no longer need to attend betrothal meetings if she found a boyfriend, so the princess had needed to introduce her to one right away—her mother wasn't going to buy that so easily.

But Alice couldn't back down now.

"Don't you have other photos? Like of his face?"

"I do not."

"Why not?"

"There's a good reason for that. He only takes photos from behind because he has such a high status that even I can hardly stand next to him."

"…What?!" The queen was shocked. "You've found a boyfriend who's *that* important?"

"Yes, I have, Mother."

That was patently false. In actuality, Rin had simply taken a picture of him as he was leaving after he and Alice had met in the neutral city. Since they couldn't let Iska find out about the photo, they'd had to take it from far away as well.

"Right, Rin? Isn't that how it is?"

"Yes. If the two of them were to so much as walk beside one another, we would have a great problem. Especially since he is an Imperial soldier—"

"Rin, don't talk about that."

She stopped her attendant from revealing more. Regardless, with Rin supporting her, the queen was slowly becoming more and more convinced.

"Then, Alice, is the reason why you're so far apart because…"

"Yes. I cannot even walk beside him, considering my social standing."

Which was true—since he was an enemy. But Alice stopped herself from revealing that tidbit and continued, "See, look, Mother. Look at his back. He practically exudes dignity from behind, does he not?"

"…Does he?" The queen peered at the photo again. "His back looks normal to me."

"Your Majesty! See, right here. There is a bright light coming from his back!"

"...Now that you mention it, I suppose he does have something of an aura radiating around him, yes."

"That's just the evening glow of the sunset—urk."

"Rin, shush." Alice held her hand over her attendant's mouth. "I met him in a neutral city. I have my heart set on him as my (battle) partner!"

"You're already that certain?!"

The queen was so shocked by her daughter's bold declaration that her eyes widened.

"I am serious, Mother. Just thinking of him, makes me burn with passion (to fight)."

"Oh my!"

The queen felt such fervor coming from Alice that she backed away. She hadn't the faintest clue that her daughter was hiding such a passionate affair from her.

"Alice, I had no idea you'd fallen so deeply in love...but wait. We cannot accept him into this country simply because he is of high status."

The Sovereignty was currently at war with the Empire. In order to become Alice's boyfriend, he needed to be able to protect himself.

"How powerful is he? Does he know how to fight, for example?"

"Rest assured that Rin can attest to his strength. Isn't that right, Rin?"

"Huh?" Alice pointed at her attendant, whose eyes had gone wide. "Rin once challenged him and was beaten to a pulp."

"Why must you bring up something that will only hurt my pride?!"

"But it is the truth."

"Urk?!...I-it is. He's powerful enough that I stood no chance against him."

Even though he's our enemy, Rin added under her breath, but it seemed the queen hadn't heard that.

"I see. So he's powerful enough to even defeat Rin. And he is of high social status, to the point even you do not feel equal to him..."

"That's right. And if I must add..."

She gulped.

...Th-this is all a sham.

...I'm doing this just to convince my mother.

Though Alice told herself that, she could feel her face heating up.

"He has...h-he has even held me in his arms!"

"He has *what*?!"

"Wait, Lady Alice?!"

Both the queen and Rin cried out.

"Lady Alice, what in the world are you saying?!"

"I'm not lying."

Though it'd only happened by coincidence when Alice and Iska had their first battle.

"And I have something more to reveal, Mother. We have even watched an opera sitting side by side (by coincidence) and (even more coincidentally) shared a meal at the same table!"

"Oh my!"

This time, the queen was so shocked, she couldn't say another word.

"Alice...when did you grow up so fast? No, I suppose I should be proud of this as your mother. Also, I cannot imagine you would do this, but have you kissed him?"

"Never! We're enemies!"

"Enemies?"

"Oh…th-that was nothing." She turned her face, which was red as a cherry, away. "Anyway, Mother, please make good on your promise."

"I see. All right then, Alice. It seems that I underestimated you."

A smile flitted across the queen's face. Alice assumed that was the smile of a mother happy about her daughter's growth, but she quickly found that she was mistaken.

"I cannot simply stand by! The ministers! Where are the ministers!" she turned and called out. "Please find a wedding venue immediately. Actually, we should really make an entirely new one. Please begin designing one today."

"Uh, um, Mother?"

But she had already left Alice to her own devices and was starting a project that her daughter hadn't even dreamed of.

"Umm, Mother?"

"We must call in journalists. The people must be informed of this joyous news. The Second Princess Aliceliese has a lover. Please make an urgent report to the news providers!"

"Please stop!"

Alice did all she could to try and stop her unexpectedly doting mother.

Several days later.

Imperial base.

"Hey, Commander Mismis, what happened to that thing you were talking about?"

"Hm?"

"You know, that rumor. That the Nebulis princess has a lover."

Iska had caught Commander Mismis napping lazily at the conference room table.

"You know, the one with the boyfriend who looks like me that you were talking about."

"Oh…I'm surprised you remember that."

"Well, I'm curious now because you said I look like him."

He hadn't heard anything since then. Iska had thought it was odd since there wasn't a commotion at headquarters.

"That's not a thing anymore."

"Huh?"

"Apparently, it really was just some rumor. The Sovereignty had jumped to conclusions, but the Empire doesn't have any details."

"…Oh."

He was relieved. He'd been worried that the Empire would begin to suspect him of something.

"And they also concluded that the guy from the rumor just looks a whole lot like you."

"See, I told you," Iska declared, full of confidence, to Commander Mismis as she was sprawled on the table. "It couldn't have been me in that picture."

File XX

Our First Meeting

Secret File

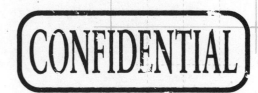

1

"Wait! Master, I said wait!"

As he exhaled, his breath white, the black-haired boy named Iska chased after a man who was already leaving. The terminal station of the continental railway was dyed in the colors of the sunset. As the travelers passed each other in the corridor, Iska couldn't catch up no matter how quickly he ran. He simply couldn't match the man's pace. Compared to the eleven-year-old boy, the man who he'd called "master" was one hundred and ninety centimeters tall.

"You always do stuff like this and then leave me behind!"

"…"

The man stopped in his tracks and whipped around.

"Leave behind? Who leaves who behind?"

"You! You leave me behind!"

"…"

"You haven't noticed?"

"I was just lost in my thoughts."

The boy sighed. Iska slumped when his teacher showed no admission of wrongdoing. This was how he always acted.

His master was a carefree wanderer who always had his head in the clouds. And whenever Iska thought the man was going to tell him something meaningful, he would always receive some half-baked response instead.

But this man was also the strongest swordsman in the Empire.

Crossweil Nes Lebeaxgate.

He stood there, his long coat covering his slim figure—not a single bit of excess fat on his body. In the past, when he had led the Saint Disciples, his moniker had been the Black Steel Gladiator, but he rarely spoke of those times now.

According to the man himself, it wasn't that he was reluctant to talk about that period in his life so much as he simply couldn't be bothered.

"So, what were you thinking about anyway?"

"About these trains."

Crossweil was staring at the brusque black trains lined up at the platform. The locomotives went to destinations all over the world.

"This one will leave in fifteen minutes. And we're getting on it."

"Okay."

"I was running a simulation in my mind of what to do if a dastardly crime syndicate decided to run amok on the train."

"But that would never happen!"

"I also thought of how I would deal with a meteor suddenly falling on the train as it was in motion—"

"Please at least base your thoughts on things that could be realistic!"

"Trying to predict what could happen is of utmost importance."

He looked incredibly serious as he said this.

"You should hypothesize what would happen if the most unfortunate and inconvenient situations were to occur. At least a few of them *will* actually occur. Whether or not you are on the battlefield, or it could happen to one of your friends if not to you."

"......Yes, sir."

Although the ideas had stemmed from absurdities, his teacher had somehow ended the lesson with a somewhat decent conclusion. That was usually how conversations with him went.

"The special express train will soon be departing for Vale Republic. Ticketholders are advised to board as they wait for departure."

"Say, Master?" As Iska listened to the announcement, he looked up at the man. "Why are we getting on a train?"

Iska still had no idea even whether they were heading out for vacation or a tour of duty.

He was suddenly told the day before that they would be going on a trip, which he'd been fine preparing for, but he still had yet to learn what his master was hoping to accomplish—as per usual.

"I've left Jhin to watch over things at home."

"Am I going to be training outside of the Empire, then...?"

"This has nothing to do with your training."

What?

As he'd lived with a grueling training regimen on a daily basis, Iska had assumed that what awaited him at the end of the trip was another frightening exercise.

"What are we going to do once we leave the Empire?" Iska asked.

"We're going to learn what it's like outside," the man replied.

"What good does knowing *that* do?"

"..."

The strongest swordsman in the Empire looked up at the station's ceiling.

"We're doing this because you have yet to learn what a witch really is," he said.

"...I know a little bit," Iska countered.

There wasn't a single person in the Empire who didn't know what a witch was. They were former humans who had been possessed by the inexplicable energy known as astral power. Witches were terrifying beings and were capable of using astral power as they desired.

They were wicked, aggressive, and loathed the Empire. Such was Iska's impression. Now, this was only his impression because Iska had never spoken to a witch himself. He had learned everything he knew of them through word of mouth.

"I wouldn't say that you've got the wrong idea about witches," the man said, "but that isn't all there is to them."

His master looked around at the people walking through the station.

"The stories passed down in the Empire about witches only apply to a minority—with exceptions like the Grand Witch Nebulis. Ninety percent of witches aren't much different from your average human. Iska, what do you think of the people walking around in this station?"

"They look like normal people to me..."

He saw businessmen boarding their trains and families on outings. They all looked like ordinary people to him.

"It's highly likely there are witches and sorcerers among them. But everyone looks exactly the same as your average Imperial. Do any of them look wicked to you?"

"No."

"So, this is just as true as all the other stories told in the Empire. Everything you're taking in with your eyes right now is real. You'll do well to keep both sides in mind."

"……Got it."

After falling silent for a while, Iska nodded.

Witches were frightening. Of course, he tried his best to take in his master's teachings, but Iska still couldn't toss aside the preconceptions he'd developed from being born and raised in the Empire.

"You'll learn eventually," the man said. "That's the whole reason we've traveled out this far."

His teacher walked ahead of him.

He was heading toward the train platform.

"Hm?"

But then his comm at his chest rang. After glancing at the name shown on the device, his master—who rarely did such a thing—clucked his tongue.

"…Why am I getting a call from such a nuisance?"

"Master, who is it? Is it Jhin?"

"Unfortunately, not. Iska, you get on the train ahead of me… What do you want, Yunmelngen? Don't push your menial tasks onto me at a time like this."

He walked away while talking to someone on the other end of the comm. It seemed he didn't want others to hear, as he walked to a far corner of the platform.

"Master? C'mon, Master! Fine, I'll get on ahead of you, then."

He walked toward the special express train for Vale Republic. Once he found two window seats, Iska sat down to claim them.

"He's really taking a long time on the phone. Will he make it in time?"

They were five minutes away from departure. Iska absent-mindedly looked through the window as he leaned back into the seat.

"…He sure is taking a while."

━━━━━━━

"The express train will soon be departing for the Graf city ruins. Ticketholders are advised to board as they wait for departure."

"Iska? Hey, Iska?"

As the announcement echoed, Iska's teacher, Crossweil, searched the inside of the train. He couldn't find any sign of his pupil. The free seating section consisted of several train cars, so it would be difficult to find someone, but it was unusual for Iska not to appear when called for so many times.

"Maybe he's waiting for me outside of the train still?"

Just in case, he got off the train. In that same moment, the express train in the next platform began to move. He watched it leave…

"Huh! Iska…?!"

Crossweil widened his eyes.

It was the train heading to Vale Republic. And in the window, he saw a black-haired boy who looked just like Iska.

"Iska!"

By the time he let out a panicked shout, it was already too late. The express train his pupil had boarded had already taken off and was chugging along toward a faraway land.

"…That dolt." He put his hand to his temple as he let out a

long sigh. "I tried simulating everything that could go wrong, but I hadn't anticipated this."

That fool of a pupil.

Apparently, he'd never considered that Iska would board the wrong train.

2

"...He sure is taking a while." Iska stifled a yawn.

He'd been waiting for his master a whole hour now. They'd long since left the terminal station, and the window now showed a view of the vast wilder lands.

"Oh, I know what happened."

After coming up with a possibility, Iska leaped from his seat.

"He must be trying to make me worry on purpose. So, where could he be hiding?"

He was used to his teacher creating problems for him to solve on a whim. This had to be another one. He probably hadn't shown up because this was his way of telling Iska to go find him.

"Seriously...Master, there's no use hiding. There aren't a lot of places to hide on this train, anyway!"

He set out walking. He headed through the cars with free seating, then to the reserved seats, checking the riders' faces as he wandered deeper into the locomotive.

In that moment, golden strands of hair flitted right by Iska's nose.

They'd passed by each other.

"..."

When Iska turned around, he found a girl with brilliant

golden hair standing right in front of him. She seemed to be eleven years old—or she might have been twelve.

So she was around his age. She had a charming and shapely face like a beautifully constructed doll, and the clothes she wore seemed tidy and of high quality. She wasn't like him, with his rumpled clothes that had been reworn many times over and were losing their shape.

That girl had stopped the moment they'd passed by each other and was now looking straight at him.

They stared at each other in silence for a while.

He wondered who she was.

Maybe she thought he was suspicious? Perhaps she was staring at him because he looked too poor to afford a ticket in the reserved section, which was unofficially closed to those without the appropriate one.

He needed to leave before she called in the conductor.

After coming to that conclusion, Iska turned his back to her and began to walk away. He needed to find his master, after all.

———

The black-haired boy turned his back to her. He walked off, heading farther into the train before she could even address him. He'd passed by her initially, so he likely was heading off to another train car with a purpose.

"…He left."

She watched him until his back disappeared from view and she heard a set of footsteps behind her.

"Lady Alice."

"…"

"Lady Alice, you cannot continue to do this. Please do not leave your seat on your own."

"Listen, listen, Lenlen!"

Alice turned around abruptly and latched onto the adult she'd called Lenlen. They weren't mother and daughter. Rather, the woman was her attendant. Alice was a princess of the Nebulis Sovereignty, the Paradise of Witches, and the woman was serving as her guard.

"Lady Alice, I was worried about you."

As the girl hugged her, Lenlen stroked Alice's hair. The woman was wearing glasses as part of her disguise, and she had on a thick winter coat to conceal the weapons in her clothes.

"My, Lady Alice, you always wander off the moment I take my eyes off of you."

"Lenlen, listen! This is more important!"

Alice herself seemed to pay no mind to Lenlen's words. It seemed her great "discovery" was taking up all her attention.

"There was a boy!"

"Excuse me?"

"He was the same age as me. He passed right by me!"

"I see… So that is what you mean."

As Alice became worked up, the guard's face softened, and her lips curled into a smile.

Aliceliese Lou Nebulis IX had no boys her age around her. All of the other children she knew were girls. As she also had a private tutor and did not attend school, she had no opportunities to speak to boys like normal girls her age. Running into a boy her age was a special occasion for her.

"Um, so, Lenlen, I was being really sneaky when I was looking at him. But then he turned around and looked back at me!"

"That must be because you are so pretty, Lady Alice."

"...Maybe I should have said something to him."

"I am not sure I can approve of that. Now, Lady Alice, this way."

The guard motioned for Alice to follow her with her hand.

All the seats around them were empty, but this was because Lenlen had bought them.

"If by some chance, anyone learns of your identity, we will have quite the commotion on our hands," Lenlen whispered. "We are currently on a trip because of a situation that came up, and I am your only guard, so we must avoid the danger of any Imperial forces finding us."

The train was headed to Vale Republic. Though the neutral country had no ties to the Empire, it was a fact that the forces had intelligence operations stationed all throughout the world.

"You wouldn't want to be chased through the streets as people call you a witch, now would you, Lady Alice?"

"It'll be fine, Lenlen. My astral power is amazing!" Alice cast Lenlen's worries aside as she proudly puffed out her chest. "I could take care of the Imperial forces with one shot of my powers. Even Mother says they're incredible."

"Yes. However, Her Majesty also said that you shouldn't use your powers yet. At least not until you have full control over them."

"...She did say that."

"It is nothing to be embarrassed about. That only serves as greater evidence that your powers are strong, and you need time to learn how to control them."

Though it was true that Princess Alice had formidable astral power, she had trouble keeping it under control. If worst came to worst and she had to fight an Imperial soldier, there was a chance she would end up freezing not only the soldier with her powers, but also buildings and innocent bystanders.

"Though it is not anywhere near how Imperials view us, there are some people in the neutral countries who fear astral mages. And if you hurt them with your powers..."

"...They would be scared of me?"

"Yes. And that would isolate us from the other countries in the world. We are forbidden from using our powers outside of the battlefield, especially within cities."

"...I understand." Alice was deeply aware that her abilities were a double-edged sword.

As soon as she first learned how to use them, she had innocently attempted to sneakily freeze a bit of the ground and ended up turning the palace's vast inner courtyard into an ice sculpture. She'd even caught an entire van and motorcycle that had been parked in the garden. Luckily, no one had been hurt, but the fear Alice had felt that day taught her that astral powers weren't simply a convenient skill to have.

"...Should I read a book until the train arrives?"

"I think that would be for the best."

"...Can I walk around the train every once in a while?"

"Please refrain from doing that, if you would. I understand you're curious about other kids your age after passing by that boy, but you should not." After she chided Alice, Lenlen broke out into an abrupt smile. "Then again, you really should have some kids your age as playmates. A boy might be an issue, but I see nothing wrong with befriending a girl."

"...Like who?"

"I have a niece who is just a year off from your age. Her name is Rin, and she's dedicated herself to her studies since she was young to serve the Lou family."

"Rin?"

"Yes. She is hoping to finish her training early and is looking forward to serving you, Lady Alice—" But Lenlen's voice was drowned out. A shrill siren had begun to go off within the entire train. "Huh? What's going on?!"

Lenlen stood up from her seat. She had her hand within her clothes, likely so she could produce her hidden weapons at any time.

There was a commotion. The passengers sitting a way off from Alice and Lenlen had begun to feel uneasy about the sudden alarm and were beginning to stand up from their seats as well.

"Lenlen, I've heard this sound in the palace, too."

"Yes, Lady Alice. But the ones you've heard there are for disaster drills in case the Imperial forces invade. This is certainly a real alarm."

"...Is it the Imperial forces?"

"No. I doubt it."

Had the forces attacked in order to target Alice?

That was unlikely. The continental railroad was a demilitarized zone through a worldwide arrangement. The forces were unlikely to break the agreement so easily.

In which case, what had triggered this alarm?

"To the Vale Republic-bound passengers of car number three, this is an emergency alert. This train is presently traveling due east through the Galato Plains—"

The PA system had turned on. All the passengers, including Alice and Lenlen, had gone quiet.

"A pack of large predators known as rexes are approaching us. We believe the pack traveled from the far south of the plains to the north."

"...Rexes?!" someone shouted.

Large predators hailing from unexplored parts of the world were generally called wilderbeasts, and rexes were a classic example of such monsters. These beasts inhabited the vast continent and were both ferocious and belligerent. They tended to attack anything in front of their eyes that moved.

And it seemed that they were after the train.

"But please rest assured that some excellent hunters are riding on this train today. Everyone, please remain cal—"

But a roar drowned out the announcement.

The windowpanes audibly cracked. Alice felt a shock wave run through the train as though something rammed itself into them. Then, finally, she heard the war cry of a ferocious beast.

3

The windows had been smashed to pieces. And then the wall behind Iska had caved in with a muffled creaking sound.

"Eep?!"

"They're here! Did they ram into us?!"

Everyone was far from calm.

After all, the train windows had been smashed to smithereens and the rexes' savage claws were flickering in and out of view in the dark of night. They were surrounded.

"The hunters! Where are the hunters?!"

"Farther back! Let's run to that train car!"

The passengers began to scramble to save themselves. They all evacuated into the next car, not even stopping to collect their luggage. By the time he came to his senses, Iska realized he'd been left alone in the train car.

"...Rexes?" Iska murmured, and at the same time, he heard the deafening sounds of gunshots ring out.

That had to be the hunters' machine guns. Beyond the shattered glass, he saw the sparks of light from the gunfire. However, the large beasts stood stark against the night, towering at five meters tall. It hadn't worked. In fact, the barrage of gunfire and subsequent pain from their wounds seemed to have made them angrier.

"That's not gonna work...!"

It was only a matter of time until they invaded the train cars.

As Iska shuddered at the thought, his mind turned not to the hunters, but the Empire's strongest swordsman, who should have been on the train.

"Master, what are you doing right now...?!"

His teacher hadn't appeared even with this commotion. Or perhaps he was already fighting against the rexes? The only thing Iska knew for certain was that the swordsman was not here with him now. He was on his own.

"You should hypothesize what would happen if the most unfortunate and inconvenient situations were to occur."

"At least a few of them will actually occur. Whether or not you are on the battlefield."

"Agh! He only gets it right at times like these!"

Iska opened his travel bag.

He unwrapped several layers of cloth from a sword made for self-defense. He doubted he could stand up against a rex with this, but it was the only thing he had on him that could be deemed a weapon.

"...I need to keep it together."

He gripped the sword as he looked around.

This wasn't the type of scenario he could go into without a plan.

He needed to protect himself while saving the passengers and driving away the rexes. In order to do all of that, Iska needed to put himself in a position where he'd be at an advantage.

"Where can I go...?"

Creak.

The wall of the train car was dented in the shape of sharp claws. The rexes had likely sunk their teeth into the train cars and were holding on with their claws. As he pictured it...

"That's right. From the rooftop...!" Iska shouted and leaped out of the train car with the force of a whirlwind.

He headed to the couplings that joined them together. After climbing up a ladder, he jumped onto the roof.

"Guh..."

The evening winds whipped past him. He was on top of the speeding train—a dangerous position where if he slipped, he'd end up falling to the ground, but this was the ideal spot.

"There!"

He ran straight across the roof to the edge of the train car and swung his sword.

"Hgh!"

He heard a rex roar. As he ran, Iska had sliced through another rex's claws. They'd been embedded in the train's walls, and by cutting them off, the rex had lost its grip and tumbled off.

One down.

"...This could work!"

Rexes were large predators. Because of that, they pounced on the train like it was their prey by instinct. All Iska had to do was cut off their claws and they'd fall right down.

"C'mon! I can even deal with four of you!"

As the wind rushed past him, he shouted so loudly, his throat went hoarse. He was doing that to encourage himself—he was scared. Because he'd practiced with his master, he was used to fighting humans more than he liked. He hadn't fought a gigantic predator before. As a child at eleven years old, a bloodthirsty rex was a monster much too big for him.

"Huh!" The strong wind carried the sound of a high-pitched scream, and Iska turned around. "...That car over there!"

As he was buffeted by the wind, he ran across the roof and jumped onto the next train car.

There it was.

A rex was attempting to clamber onto the roof. When the beast saw Iska, it roared intimidatingly, but he rushed at it, pushing off from the floor to go even faster. He couldn't be frightened. He had to protect the train. If the beasts successfully climbed on, they could get to the engine car and stop the train completely. If that happened, all the passengers would become prey to the beasts.

"No way. I will not let you make it up here!"

He devoted himself to brandishing his sword. He cut the beast's claws with a single swing and the second rex fell.

"...Tsk...haah..."

He'd only been fighting for a few minutes, but he was panting unbelievably hard. It wasn't simple fatigue either. The pressure from this life-or-death situation was making it difficult to breathe.

"Where next?! The front?!"

He had to rely on his ears rather than his eyes in the darkness. He started running in the direction he thought the rexes would be.

"There!"

He swung his sword at the faintly illuminated carnivore. However...

"Ouch?!"

Iska was the one to cry out. A dull pain ran through him like electricity as his wrist to his elbow went numb and stopped working.

His sword had been sent flying. The rex had sensed Iska coming and kicked up its front leg at its prey—in other words, Iska. He had barely managed to defend himself with his sword.

"Guh..."

But now his right arm refused to move.

"...Just fall!"

He grabbed his sword with his left hand and once again sliced at the rex holding on to the train.

That made three.

Behind Iska, he heard the sweeping fire of a machine gun.

"...There's more at the last car!"

He didn't even have time to catch his breath as he leaped across the extremely unsteady train cars, heading farther down.

Iska had yet to notice in the darkness that a small crack had formed in his sword.

＝＝＝＝＝＝＝＝＝

"It's gotten through the window and is in the train!"

"The tenth car is a lost cause! We need to disconnect it! Evacuate to the ninth car right now!"

Bzzt...

Lights violently flickered in the train car as the rexes that had caught up to the caboose snapped through the cables one after another.

Alice hadn't seen the disaster herself, but she knew exactly how dire the situation was based on the strained cries of the hunters.

"..."

She cowered in her seat. Just as the hunters had ordered, Alice and the other passengers nearby were sitting and keeping silent as they waited. The hunters had said that would be the safest.

....

...*But is it really?*

Alice didn't understand the adults' plan.

As she stayed perfectly still, she began to wonder whether she was doing the right thing. Emotions began to bubble up from within her.

After all, Alice had a power that could save them from this situation—she had immense astral power. Her single worry was whether she would lose control of it since she knew the power was dangerous and even her mother had forbidden her from using it. But if she *could* control it, she'd be able to save the passengers.

"...Lenlen! Um, Lenlen."

The moment she tried to talk to the guard next to her, she heard the crunch of metal. The windowpanes broke, and shards flew at them as a rex arm as thick as a log swung into the car.

The predator outside was groping for the humans in the train car.

"Huh!"

Alice felt a chill run down her spine. Her astral power had activated half unconsciously as the enemy closed in on her in front of her eyes.

"You mustn't, Lady Alice!"

As she stood up, Lenlen gripped her arm, trying to tell her not to use her power. Alice could see in Lenlen's eyes exactly what the guard wanted to say, even if it wasn't put into words. She understood, but the screams from the passengers only continued to grow louder.

"N-noooo?!"

"Get back! Damn it! Are they trying to get into this car, too?!"

Alice heard a mother with her kids scream from close by. The hunters who had come running over showered the rexes that were clinging to the walls with a barrage of bullets.

"Lady Alice," Lenlen was murmuring, though her voice was drowned out by the din of the gunfire. "Lady Alice, your intentions are noble, and I am painfully aware of exactly what you wish to do."

"…"

"But please not right now. I do not mean to be insolent, but your astral powers have the potential to bring about more casualties than the rexes."

"……I know."

And how frustrating it was to the princess—to the astral mage. Even though she had the power to solve the problem they were in, because she was so inexperienced at controlling it, she was powerless to do anything.

No, she wasn't entirely powerless. She was frustrated because she had been told not to act and had no argument to justify helping.

"Leave it up to the hunters."

"…But!"

Alice pointed at the crushed window frame and didn't hold back her howl. They were at their limit—the passengers, the hunters, and the train itself.

"The window is broken! And there are more and more rexes leaping onto the train. They're on the roof and are closing in… Wait…"

She doubted her eyes. Beyond the window that Alice pointed

to, a rex had fallen from the roof. Had it simply lost balance? But then another fell in front of Alice in the same way as she pondered over what was happening.

Was it the hunters? No, the hunters already had their hands full protecting them inside of the train. They couldn't have been outside.

"…Is there someone on the roof?"

She slowly approached the window. She placed a hand on the unbroken window glass and looked up outside the car.

"Lady Alice! You must get away from the window!"

"…"

Lenlen's shout never reached Alice's ears. She was fully preoccupied by the scene outside the car she was witnessing playing out in front of her.

From the top of the roof…

…a boy with black hair and a small sword was striking down rexes one after another as Alice watched.

"It's the boy from before!"

She was absolutely stunned. It was the same boy she had passed by in the afternoon. In the intense cold night, he was singlehandedly fighting off the pack of rexes attempting to scale the train.

"…But that's so dangerous!"

It was entirely different from attempting to shoot them from afar. On the unsteady roof, the boy used a small sword to attack the rexes directly. Just imagining the feat sent a shiver through Alice. She was so scared; she could never do that. Even the adult hunters would have likely been paralyzed from fear. How could a boy like him put up such a fight on his own?

No, it wasn't a matter of *how* the boy could do it—the issue was why *she* wasn't doing anything. That was what was central to her internal conflict—because she knew she should be able to do something. As a princess of astral mages, hadn't this power been given to her for exactly a time like this?

"…Huh!"

When Alice saw the boy bend back slightly, she was instantly brought back to the present.

His sword had broken.

The blade had snapped in half when he failed to dodge a rampaging rex, and the boy fell over as his weapon was knocked out of his hands.

And the rex that had clambered onto the roof was closing in on him, ready to attack…

"No!"

"Lady Alice?!"

Alice jumped out of the train without thinking.

She had pushed away Lenlen's arm and passed by the gun-toting hunters, weaving through the other passengers.

She headed to the couplings that held the train cars together.

Alice, out of breath, reached outside and looked up right as two rexes hurled themselves at the boy who had lost his sword.

She realized there was no time to hesitate. If she did, he would be dead.

And so…

"Please, astral power!"

She was fully absorbed in commanding the astral power that dwelled within her. What she had pictured was an ice shield. She couldn't allow her power to go out of control. She prayed that the boy wouldn't be hurt by the cold.

She begged the astral power.

"Protect him!"

As the chill spread, it glittered a bright blue.

A wall of ice, clear as crystal had formed out of nowhere, suddenly towering over the rexes and deflecting their attack. It was like a shield of ice.

"......Huh?"

Iska's vision grew blurry from the blood weeping from his forehead, but he blinked in surprise.

What in the world had happened?

The sword he had gotten from his master had broken, and Iska himself had been injured by the rexes' attacks. But just as he'd been cornered, this ice wall had appeared out of nowhere.

"Get down!"

"Huh!"

A delicate voice that the wind nearly carried away shouted. Iska had no idea who the speaker was, but he knelt over as cold objects whizzed by him overhead one after another.

They were bits of hail.

As the pebbles hit the rexes almost like bullets, the beasts fell down.

"Was that astral power?!"

The roof of the train was deathly silent.

By the time Iska turned around in a panic, the person had already disappeared from behind him. There was no way hail could have suddenly fallen from the sky right in that moment. He knew it must have been astral power. It seemed a rather powerful witch had happened to be on the same train as him.

And that person had driven away the rexes.

"…Was I saved…?"

No longer driven by a desperate need to survive, Iska collapsed on the spot.

He hadn't simply broken his sword. He had used up all his stamina and his ability to pay attention to anything around him. He was in a dangerous state.

"……It couldn't be…"

He couldn't believe he'd been saved.

But more importantly…

He couldn't believe a witch would protect an Imperial like him.

It was a coincidence.

The witch probably never would have imagined that a boy so far from home could be an Imperial.

"…But."

Regardless, the fact still remained that he had been saved by a witch.

The witches the Empire had taught him about were wicked and cruel—and he never would have believed one would use her powers to save the passengers or himself.

"So, this is just as true as all the stories told in the Empire. Everything you're taking in with your eyes right now is real."

"You'll do well to keep both sides in mind."

"Master…is this…?"

Iska turned around.

He no longer heard the hunters' guns and all signs of the rexes had disappeared as though they'd never been there.

"Oh......"

He saw the dark horizon. Iska finally realized the dim light ahead was the light of a city. They had arrived.

They were at the Graf city ruins.

4

"You got on the train to the Vale Republic."

"No way!"

He was on the platform at the station the train pulled into.

Iska had shouted when he'd heard the first thing his master said—his teacher who had arrived earlier than him.

"I had to follow you that entire distance on another train. But yours ended up slowing down so much, I made it here ahead of you."

His master sighed upon seeing the train Iska had been on.

The windows were cracked in places, and the outer walls had graphic vestiges of the rexes' claws.

"Looks like you put on quite the race."

His master's eyes landed on Iska's broken blade, which the boy still clutched.

"What happened to that?"

"It broke."

"'It broke'? You must have abused it, then."

He showed Iska no sympathy whatsoever—or so Iska thought until the greatest swordsman in the Empire said, quite loquaciously and uncharacteristically, "You bungled it, but you didn't do the wrong thing."

"......Huh?"

"A sword is tool to be used. It's okay to break a national trea-sure or even a sword inscribed with the name of a blacksmith—as long as you're doing it to save someone."

"Are you praising me right now?"

"Yes, for what you're currently capable of."

Iska felt relieved. It seemed that fighting off the rexes had bal-anced out any lecture he would have gotten about boarding the wrong train or breaking his sword.

"Oh…but, Master, I didn't actually fight off the rexes."

"It was the hunters, right?"

"Actually, it wasn't them either…"

"Huh?"

"Uh, I'm not sure how to explain this but…"

I was saved by a witch.

Reporting that was simple enough, but he felt frustrated that he hadn't seen her face or known who she was.

Just who had saved him?

"…A lot of things happened."

"How was I supposed to know that, you fool?"

While the two of them were talking, some distance away…

"I wonder where that boy went?"

"What is it, Lady Alice?"

"Nothing…nothing at all."

The girl with the golden hair held on to her guard's hand as they left the platform.

That moment of their encounter had resulted in the Black Steel's Successor, Iska, rethinking his view on witches.

And it was also when the Ice Calamity Witch, Alice, had

vowed to make her secret ability her ice flower—in other words, her shield.

But little did the two of them know that it had also been the moment their fates were sealed.

Secret

*Or the Reunion the World
Knows Not Of*

Our Last CRUSADE OR THE RISE OF A New World
Secret File

Imperial capital.

The utopia powered by machines, the Empire's core.

It was the land where, about a century prior, the first gigantic geyser of astral energy—a vortex—had been discovered. Though the city had been reduced to ash by the Founder Nebulis, it was reborn as a city of steel.

And this was the innermost area of the Imperial capital.

The topmost floor of the four buildings, the Heaven of Insight and Nonsight.

"**Hwaaah.**" A silver beastperson stifled back a small yawn.

The beast's entire body was covered in a thick coat of fur like a fox's, but their face was oddly friendly and resembled something between that of a girl's and a cat's. Their eyes were large as a kitten's, and though sharp fangs protruded from the corners of their mouth, there was something charming about that.

An inhuman beast.

How shocked would the citizens of the Empire be if they were to learn this was Lord Yunmelngen?

Even the Lord's direct guards, the Saint Disciples, were only allowed an audience through a thin cloth curtain. This person held supreme authority over the Empire and was the nation's greatest secret.

"It happened years ago."

The Lord sat cross-legged on top of a space covered in tatami mats, relaxing.

Clack.

Clack.

The Lord was playing an old board game called sengi by themselves.

"You told me about it before, didn't you? When your silly pupil got on the wrong intercontinental train, and it was attacked by a stampede of wilderbeasts."

"I don't remember that."

The voice had come from the entrance.

Though the Lord only had visitors from outside once in many years, their eyes remained on the board game in front of them.

"You already forgot? You told me about it yourself back then. That a powerful witch happened to be on that train. You had me look into her, too."

"And?"

"You were right."

The Lord pushed the piece on the board that read "queen" forward, their sharp claws flicking in and out of view.

The Sovereignty and the Empire.

The Lord moved both sides all on their own.

"The current queen...uh, I believe she's the eighth right now? Her daughter just so happened to be out on an excursion at the time. She was riding on the same train as your foolish pupil. Don't you want to know her name?"

"You called me over here just for that?"

"What else would I call you for?"

Lord Yunmelngen raised their head.

It had been years since the man had appeared before the Lord.

The former Saint Disciple of the first seat, Crossweil Nes Lebeaxgate, was there.

The Lord's former guard. The man had retired from his post some ten odd years ago, and left the Lord.

"Crow, where have you been wandering lately?"

"..."

The former Saint Disciple—or Crow, as he'd been called—let out a small sigh.

"The astrals had a request for me."

"Then you must have come a long way. Have you finished that business?"

"Only partially."

"You should hurry."

The beastperson raised themself to one knee.

"Nebulis will soon grow impatient and awaken. She'll likely respond to the astral swords."

"Very likely."

"How troublesome. All she can think of is taking revenge on the Empire."

The Lord shook their head heavily. For a moment, they squinted nostalgically at the tall man who looked down upon them.

"She's your sister, isn't she? You really ought to do something about her this time."

"I gave up on that a century ago."

He looked resigned as he—the Black Steel Gladiator

Crossweil—answered Lord Yunmelngen without any emotion in his voice.

"If I make a move, it'll be like adding fuel to the fire. I can't save this planet. I told you that when I left."

"I remember. And that you also entrusted the astral swords with another for that very reason."

"...That's right."

His black coat fluttered.

"It's time."

"Already leaving, are you?"

"I can't leave the astrals waiting. They're rather capricious."

"I see. Then off you go."

"..."

"Oh, before I forget."

The former guard was about to leave.

Until Lord Yunmelngen had stopped him—that is.

"I forgot to tell you something important."

"What?"

"It was Unit 907, wasn't it? Your foolish pupil is about to return to the Imperial capital. It seems he was in the Sovereignty for a while, but I've called him back."

"..."

"Wasn't there something you had to tell him?"

As he looked down on the beastperson smiling at him from the tatami room, Iska's teacher sighed.

"Tell me something as important as that first, will you?"

Afterword

Thank you for picking up *Our Last Crusade or the Rise of a New World: Secret File* (*Last Crusade*)!

I think this will be the first time for many of you to read the short stories of *Last Crusade*.

This is a special volume that has compiled all the *Last Crusade* short stories serialized in the bimonthly *Dragon Magazine* from Fantasia Bunko.

Normally, we'd just do a one-shot, but several people have asked for a short story collection, so that's what we went with. It's my first one, so I'd be so happy if you enjoyed it!

Also, the stories are essentially divided based on whether they take place in the Empire or Sovereignty, which is a particular feature of *Last Crusade*.

Iska, the protagonist from the Empire, and Alice, from the Sovereignty.

Because the superpowers are at war, we don't get to see the

everyday lives of Iska and Alice in the Empire and palace, so this *Secret File* goes behind the scenes of the main narrative. I was able to write about that new aspect of their lives.

So, I'll summarize each story very quickly.

◇File 01 "Or the Double Booking Duel" (September 2017)

When the second volume of the main series came out, this short story was serialized in *Dragon Magazine*.

This story was perfect for those interested in the anime, as it was focused on Iska and Alice's relationship.

A neutral city that couldn't make an appearance in the main story shows up, and it gives a peek into why witches and sorcerers are feared in *Last Crusade*, strengthening the world building.

◇File 02 "Or the Unavoidable Clash at the Bootcamp?" (July 2018)

Just what types of training do Iska and the rest of Unit 907 do?

This delves into the secrets of the Imperial forces. Though they normally have serious training sessions, at times, they're subjected to absurd exercises based on Risya or the headquarters' whims.

There are plans for Commander Pilie to appear again later, so please cheer her on if you see her again!

◇ File 03 "Or Life in a Flower Garden of Women" (May 2019)

What does Iska do when he's not training?

To address that, this story is about his busy everyday life after training drills.

All he wants to do is spend his days relaxing in the men's barracks, but Nene and Mismis generally disrupt that.

You'll also see another side of Risya that you won't see in the main story.

(Well, really that side of Risya might be the Saint Disciple in her natural element.)

◇ File 04 "Or Alice's Betrothal War (Her Happily Ever After)?" (July 2019)

Alice is in a panic in the Sovereignty.

She sends every one of her prospective suitors back to their home country unconscious...

Also, I personally like the last conversation between her and the queen.

Since the queen was a problem child in a different way from Alice during her youth, I'd like to write about that in a short story sometime. (And a certain sorcerer would appear as well.)

◇ File XX "Our First Meeting" (New story)

This is a super-secret episode that really exemplifies *Secret File*.

This is also the true version of events of the scene that appeared in a flashback at the beginning of the third chapter of the first volume of *Last Crusade*.

I hope you'll take a look at the beginning of the third chapter of the first volume again.

And also, Iska's master!

This is where the mysterious previous owner of the astral swords makes his first appearance.

There are plenty more "secrets" packed into this volume that's only made up of short stories, so I hope you enjoy them!

◇ Secret "Or the Reunion the World Knows Not Of" (New story)

This short story is an epilogue about the master and the Lord.

It seems that the Lord is very forthcoming about sharing

secrets with the master, but that's something to look forward to learning about in the main storyline.

Also, this epilogue is the most recent of the set, as far as chronological order goes. How will their reunion tie into the future of the tenth volume of the main story that's coming out next?

I hope you're looking forward to finding out!

…Now, then. That's enough about this book. Let's get into announcements next.

▼ The *Last Crusade* TV anime will be airing in October of 2020!

The broadcast date has finally been decided!

The planning took some time, but the broadcast you've been waiting for will come this October!

In addition, more details about the anime are in the process of being revealed to the public, especially about the cast.

Iska (Yusuke Kobayashi)

Aliceliese Lou Nebulis IX (Sora Amamiya)

The two voice actors from the 2018 public audio drama will be reprising their roles as the leads in the anime!

This is a very happy thing, and so reassuring.

And of course, Commander Mismis, Jhin, Nene, Rin, Risya, the queen, and also Iska and Jhin's teacher will be there!

All the important characters who made an appearance in the short story collection and the main story have started recording.

We've got a great lineup, so I hope you're looking forward to it!

So, on to the most recent bit of anime news.

The official *Our Last Crusade or the Rise of a New World* account: (https://twitter.com/kimisen_project)

Updates are planned to be posted there. I hope you'll take a look at it!

And I'd like to briefly mention my other current series.

The series currently serializing with MF Bunko J is reaching its climax.

▼ *Why Does No One Remember My World?* (*Why Does No One Remember*)

The eighth volume of the novel has been published.

The ninth volume, which will be the latest one, will be coming out soon on August 25th. The manga version is also serialized in *Monthly Comic Alive*, so I hope you'll support it, too!

Now then...

The afterword is nearing its end too, so I'd like to also take the moment to say some personal thank-yous.

To Ao Nekonabe, who drew another first-rate cover, thank you very much!

The *Dragon Magazine* cover version of Alice was super wonderful!

And also, my editor Y, who has worked with me since the sixth volume of *Last Crusade*, has been reassigned.

Though the time we worked together was short, you supported me when we met in person, during the Fantasia reader appreciation event when we made the anime announcement, at the anime script meetings, and during the very important plans regarding the anime and media franchising. I am truly grateful!

And to my new editors O and S, it was very reassuring to have you devoting your all to the short story collection and anime plans immediately after taking over from Y. I hope to work with you further for the future anime broadcast and the exciting developments of the novel!

Next is *Last Crusade* 10.

A tale about the swordsman Iska and the witch princess Alice.

A formidable enemy stands in Iska and his companions' way as they attempt to get to the Empire. Meanwhile, Alice faces off against the oldest and most powerful Grand Witch once again.

I hope you'll give your attention to the even fiercer battles that are raging between the two who have been drawn together.

Well then...

Why Does No One Remember 9 is planned to come out August 25th.

Last Crusade 10 comes out October 20th in Japan.

And...

The anime of *Last Crusade* will be released in October along with the tenth volume!

I'll work hard to make sure that both series are exciting for summer and fall of this year, so I hope you're looking forward to them!

On an evening verging on summer,

Kei Sazane

HAVE YOU BEEN TURNED ON TO LIGHT NOVELS YET?

86—EIGHTY-SIX, VOL. 1–11

In truth, there is no such thing as a bloodless war. Beyond the fortified walls protecting the eighty-five Republic Sectors lies the "nonexistent" Eighty-Sixth Sector. The young men and women of this forsaken land are branded the Eighty-Six and, stripped of their humanity, pilot "unmanned" weapons into battle...

Manga adaptation available now!

WOLF & PARCHMENT, VOL. 1–6

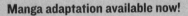

The young man Col dreams of one day joining the holy clergy and departs on a journey from the bathhouse, Spice and Wolf. Winfiel Kingdom's prince has invited him to help correct the sins of the Church. But as his travels begin, Col discovers in his luggage a young girl with a wolf's ears and tail named Myuri, who stowed away for the ride!

Manga adaptation available now!

SOLO LEVELING, VOL. 1–8

E-rank hunter Jinwoo Sung has no money, no talent, and no prospects to speak of—and apparently, no luck, either! When he enters a hidden double dungeon one fateful day, he's abandoned by his party and left to die at the hands of some of the most horrific monsters he's ever encountered.

Comic adaptation available now!